Journey of a Butterfly

By: KeArra Robinson

Dedicated To:

This book is dedicated to my family and friends. They have always supported me and pushed me to achieve my dreams and goals, no matter how big, or small they were. Their encouragement has meant so much to me. They even believed in me when I did not believe in myself. We may not be perfect, but we are perfectly imperfect.

Acknowledgements:

I want to acknowledge and give special thanks to Mary Kendrick, Cathy Tave, and Tameka Davis as they helped me develop this novel and gave me to confidence to complete it. I also want to acknowledge a classmate of mine, Jamecia Reed, who offered to edit and help me develop my book as well. She is one of the reasons I started writing. I was inspired by her short story and upcoming book, *"I Can't Touch You"*.

Table of Contents

Prologue

I rolled over to check the time. 5:04am. Before I could get myself straight, I hear it. The sound of my four-year-old son singing. Jayden was my only child. He is a brilliant kid, but he has attention deficit hyperactivity disorder.

"Jayden go back to bed baby. It's too early", I said into the mic. I kept a camera in his room. I must keep a close eye on him, sometimes Jayden has these rages and energy burst. I feel he may hurt himself.

"But mom, I can't sleep," he replied.

"Look, it's too early, and I am not about to debate with you," I said, "go back to bed."

By the time I got him back settled, it was now 6:00am. I had to get up at 7:00am to take Jayden to the bus stop, there was no reason to fall back asleep, I might as well get some work done. By work, I mean school work. I graduated high school five years ago, but I am still in college. I finally finished school for medical billing and coding degree and was now going back for my associates in healthcare management. I sat on my bed and grabbed my laptop. I tried to focus on the screen in front of me, but I just couldn't. Today was the day I had to pick up my husband's ashes. It was not like I wanted them, but I had to play the part of a grieving wife, or else something would seem off. I pushed my computer away. I wouldn't be able to focus at least not right now. I laid down and let my thoughts take over.

The Egg

My name is Kennadi Williams, everyone calls me Ke. Growing up, I lived in a little rural town called Blueville. It's located in the northeast part of Texas. They should call it Nosey Ville, everyone here knew everyone's business. I lived with my granny, everyone called her Ms. Marie, aunt Tiff, cousin Shay, and my little brother Marques, we called him Marq. My grandmother was a short little woman with a big personality. She could be your best friend but be sure never to cross her. She has no problem giving people a piece of her mind, and the apple doesn't fall far from the tree. My aunt Tiff was the same way. She tries to be nice, but her facial expression will say it all. Shay is aunt Tiff's daughter, and Marques is my little brother. Shay and I were quiet, shy people. My brother is the poster child for big things came in small packages; short little guy but was very bold. He was outgoing, friendly, and charming. Even at the age of three, he could charm the women at the grocery store. We all shared a three-bedroom, one-bathroom house. It was one house of three on the block. It was made up of brick and wood. It burned down once before, but my grandmother remodeled it and stayed. My grandmother was a divorcee. I am not sure what happened between her and my grandfather, and I never asked. My room was in the front. It was made of brick. It was an added room, it used to be the porch. There was a door still there that lead to the new porch. Across the street from us was Jade's was an old convenient store. It is still open to this day. My aunt Tiff worked there. Jade's sold snacks, medicine, other things you wanted to buy, but not travel across the tracks for, but the best item was free, entertainment. Sometimes my family and I would just look out the window if we were bored. Fights, arguments, arrest, and accidents seemed to always happen in Jade's parking lot. I loved Jade's because it allowed me to see the greatest man I knew, my grandfather, David Williams. Everyone called him Big D, I called him PaPa. My grandfather was 6'7". Seemed like a giant to me.

"Ke-Baby!" he screamed.

"PaPa," I yelled as I ran and grabbed his legs.

He always spoiled me rotten. Every time I saw him, he bought me candy or gave me money. Five bucks was a lot to a four-year-old. He ran his own towing business. He would take me to work with him and let me operate the knobs to load the cars. He was also a biker. He would travel to different states to attend field meets. I have never been to one, but I am guessing they are where biker clubs meet up and have a good time dancing and enjoying life. He was the greatest! I bet you are wondering why I haven't mentioned my mom or dad about now. Well, it, because they were not around. As for my father, he is dead. He died when I was about thirteen months old. The story I was told was my dad was playing Russian roulette. You know the game where you put one bullet in the chamber, spin the barrel, point it at your head, and pull the trigger. He was sitting on the bed playing that game, while I was laying on the bed behind him. My mom panicked and tried to grab the gun. (Pow) The gun went off in the struggle.

My father passed that night. I do not remember the funeral, but my mom told me I was crawling on his corpse during the body viewing. All I have left from my dad is a jacket he got me. It is a little burned from a fire, but I will never get rid of it. As for my mom, I have a few memories of her before Kindergarten. I remember us living in an apartment in Mesquite, me my mom and my little brother. I had to be about three at the time. I was not in school, and Marques was a baby. I was a busy body. I remember running through the house playing as my mom took care of my brother. I was playing with Ke-Op, my imaginary friend.

"Up, up, and away" I screamed. We were playing heroes. I was Catman, she was Bobin. Who said girls couldn't be superheroes? We jumped on the couch, to the floor across the room to the other couch. (Grrrrsplaaash) The sound imitated the sound a bag of glass marbles that cracked against the floor.

"What was that?" my mom screamed.

I said nothing.

She ran out of the room to find me standing in the middle of the living room where the glass table used to be. I think I was in shock because I didn't move. She picked me up and ran to the bathroom. Her hands shook as she poured alcohol onto a cotton ball and rubbed my face, it burned so bad. After this incident, I noticed my mom started taking me out of the house more. She would take me to play at the park and to play with other kids. My best friend at the time was Nadine. She was a mixed little girl that lived in our apartments. She had long curly brown hair. She had this habit of sucking her thumb, I gained that habit from her over time. It was soothing. Nadine's parents were very friendly. They always gave me candy when I came over. I would go over her house to play with dolls or try to climb trees. One day a bird fell out of its nest. Nadine and I were trying to figure out how to put it back in. Nadine started to cry.

"He's going to die if we don't help it," she cried.

"I'm trying!", I yelled. I had scratches everywhere trying to get up that tree. Nadine's dad walked up.

"What's going on here?", he said.

"Help, dad you have to save it!", she screamed.

Nadine's dad picked up the bird and put it back in its nest. Nadine was so happy, she jumped up to hug his legs. He picked her up, and they walked into the house. I went home happy for the bird, but I couldn't help but be jealous. I wish it was that simple to get picked up and put into my dad's nest. My mom took care of us the best she could, but she never seemed happy. One night her boyfriend at the time came over.

"Marvin you are not taking my son!", she yelled

"He is my son too!", he argued.

It was late in the evening, I was playing in my room and heard the argument. I peeked out my door. (Slam) They shut it.

"You need to leave!", my mom yelled.

"I'm not going anywhere," he screamed.

Well, I was. I got my shoes and left. I walked downstairs and across the street to Nadine's house. It looked like there was a party going on. Balloons were everywhere. I saw Nadine's mom and dad inside, and there was cake. I stayed outside the door Nadine came to the door, she told me she couldn't come out. Disappointed I sat on the porch.

"Why the long face?", said a tall bald man.

"Nadine can't play," I said with a shaky voice.

"It's okay, would you like to come with me and get ice cream?", he replied.

"Yes!", I said wiping the tears from my eyes. As we walked to the car. I heard someone screaming. I turned to see my mom. She ran over pushed the man and grabbed my arm. I had never seen her this mad before. She dragged me by my arm across the street and up to our apartment. She cried and yelled at me all at once.

"You are never to go with strangers, and don't you ever leave this house by yourself again!", mom exclaimed.

"Yes Mam," I sobbed.

"Now, go get my belt," she said.

Let's just say after that I never thought of leaving the house. In fact, that was the last time I saw Nadine. I was scared to get in trouble again, and shortly after the incident, we moved back to Blueville to live with my granny, and the rest of the family.

Where's Mom?

A year and a half had passed since we lived in Mesquite. I loved living with my grandma. She always made breakfast before she sent us off to school. (Yaaawwwn) I had woken to the smell of bacon. I got out of bed and proceeded to the kitchen where I found my granny cooking breakfast. All my favorites bacon, eggs, sausage, and oatmeal. I loved oatmeal. My granny always made hers with butter sugar and carnation milk. That milk made all the difference. My mom attempted to make it once, but my brother and I got sick. After breakfast, I ran to my room to put on my favorite dress. I had started kindergarten and had begun making friends. My best friend name was Aniya, I called her Niya. Our moms were best friends. They were even pregnant at the same time. We did everything together. We were known as each other's sidekicks. I grabbed my backpack and ran out of the door. My grandmother took me to school. Today was the test day. I was so excited because I could count to 100. I knew I would pass.

"I'm coming to get you early today Ke," Granny said.

"But why?", I asked.

"Not that I owe you an explanation, but we have somewhere to go," she stated.

"Yes Mam," I answered.

I wondered where we would be going. I hope it was Mac Ronald's I loved the play place. We arrived at Johnston Elementary. A small school made up of three hallways and two play areas. One was so old, it was made of wood. I rushed out of the car. I saw Niya, James, and Treveyon, I ran over to them. Treveyon and James were best friends. They were also me and Niya's "boyfriends." Last week at the kindergarten dance, we were paired to dance with each

15

other, and it kind of stuck. Niya and James, me and Treveyon, party of four. I went through the school day as usual. I aced my test, and during recess, Niya and I played "Mrs. Mary Mack." We had square pizza for lunch, and I had a quarter for an extra carton of orange juice. In Ice Block's voice, today was a good day. I loved Ice Block. He was in my favorite movie "Saturday." I knew every line in that movie by heart. My favorite character was Teebo. I would imitate him so much my grandpa took a break from calling me Ke-Baby and called me Keebo. I hope I can watch it when I get home today.

(Beep) "Mrs. Loftin?"

"Yes?"

"Could you send Kennadi to the front office, her grandmother is her to pick her up."

"Okay, she will be there in a few."

I grabbed my backpack. I was excited to tell me, grandmother, the results of my test and find out where we were going. When I approached the office, my grandmother did not look well. Her eyes were red. She signed me out, and we walked to the car. My mom was in the backseat with my brother, she didn't look well either. I gave her a hug, then buckled my seatbelt. We arrived downtown to an orange building. I recognized the building because it was across from the place, we got the hot links. We had never been there before. My granny parked the car, and we all got out.

As we entered the building, my mom had to sign some forms. My granny took us to the waiting room. There was this old tv there for people to watch. I was more interested in the glass block wall. I tried to count the blocks to see how many made up the entire wall. My mom came into the waiting room, and they began to talk. She came over to me.

16

She gave me a hug and told me she loves me and then explained that she must go away now. I didn't know what that meant exactly. She grabbed my brother and did the same thing. As she gave him back to my granny, he started to cry. Two men grabbed my mother and took her down this long hall. I just remember seeing her black floral outfit disappear.

"Ke," my granny called.

I stood there looking for my moment completely confused.

"Ke," she repeated.

"Yes?", I said.

"We have to go now," she said.

I didn't know what just happened, but it felt wrong. Something bad just happened. When we got home, my aunt was there. My granny put Marq down for a nap and sent me to watch cartoons as they talked in the kitchen. I was happy I loved watching Cows and Chickens. The theme song was fun to sing. That night we ate pizza, my granny let me get three pieces! The next morning, I woke up, I looked for my mother. She wasn't there.

"Granny where is my mom?"

"She is not home, but you will see her soon."

The next time I saw was a mom was at that orange building through a glass window. I had to talk to her through a payphone. Turns out the trail was over, it was time for her to serve her sentence related to my dad's death. I told her about school, and that granny was letting Niya spend the night that upcoming weekend. Next, my brother spoke, I did not understand a word he was saying, but it made my mother smile. My grandmother spoke last before we had to go. She kept saying everything would be okay. A woman came to talk to my mom, we had to say goodbye. We made a few visits like this until my mom was moved to a different facility. We would get letters from her every week, and my granny and aunt would take turns reading them to us. She also sent gifts. I still have the purse she crotched for me with my initials on it. As time went on, more letters came. It was nice to hear from her, but I needed to see her. I felt like something was missing.

Well, I finally got my wish. We were going to see my mom. It took about three hours to get there, but to me, it felt like eight. We pulled up to this large gated white building. As we drove to the visitor's lot, I could not help but notice the large silver pointy rope at the top of the fences. They mimicked the rings of a slinky, but they didn't look like toys. The closer we got to the parking lot, the more scared I became. There was a large field with multiple towers throughout it. They reminded me of lighthouses I saw in my books, but there was no water nearby. I don't want to go in there. The car came to a stop. My granny gave us a smoked sausage sandwich before we went in; there was no outside food allowed. As we approached the building, we walked through these massive grey beeping walls, then we were scanned by a lady's beeping wand. This place was both exciting and scary at the same time. After the lady gave my granny her keys back. We all walked over to the waiting room. My granny got us situated, while my aunt got us snacks. After a while, they called us.

"Williams family?", the lady said.

My granny raised her hand, we all walked over. She took us to the field area I saw on the way in. We sat at this white picnic bench and waited for my mom. Five minutes later she ran out to us. My brother and I ran meeting her halfway. I felt a pure rush on energy as I saw my mom. I squeezed her neck as hard as I could. She picked my brother and me up at the same time and buried her face in our shoulders. You could feel the love pour out of each of us. We held hands as we walked over to the white picnic table. My brother and I updated mom on all the things that were happening with us. Filled with excitement, we both were talking so fast telling her about our friends and our favorite colors. After we ran out of things to say, the adults started to speak. Marq and I ran all over the field getting flowers for our mom. Before we knew it, it was time to go. The next few minutes were filled with tight hugs and tear-filled goodbyes. My brother screamed and chased after her as she was led away. It took all the strength my aunt and granny had to contain him. The ride home was somber. No one really spoke, I put my arm around my brother and looked out the window, as he cried himself to sleep.

A few weeks passed before we would start this journey again, but this time it was different. We were going to be taking pictures. The night before my granny had twisted Shay and my hair, we had twisted pigtails all over our heads. My brother had got his hair cut at Mr. John's. We were dressed in our best clothes. I wore a blue sweater vest with white and light blue stripes, khaki pants, and my black baby doll shoes. After breakfast, we all piled into the van and started the journey. When we got, their things went as usual with the addition of taking a family photo. My mom's hair was cute in a short style and curled. She stood in the middle as we all surrounded her to take the picture. We talked for a while then said our goodbyes.

We piled back in the van and got on the road on the road and headed back home. About thirty minutes later, (BOOM, pop, Skurrrrrt), the van jerked. My granny fought to keep steer the van over to the side of the road. Granny and aunt Tiff got out of the vehicle; turns out our tire had popped. My granny facial expression was a picture of defeat. I could not have been easy for her to support her daughters two children on her own. Now this, she did not have any money to repair a car. Her only other support was her daughter Tiff, and she did not have much to spare either. They both returned to the vehicle to try to think of a plan. My granny eyes teared up as she ran out of options.

A white 1980s Honda Civic pulled up behind us: an older tall, slender man got out. He approached the driver door. The window was already down because it was so hot.

"Do y'all need help?"

He had a southern accent more distinct than ours. It sounded like he was from Louisiana than Texas.

My granny shook her head yes. "We were trying to get home when our tire blew out."

"Where ya going?", he asked.

"Blueville, it's about an hour north of Dallas."

"Alright, I will take you," he replied.

My granny paused for a moment in disbelief. "Are you sure?" She explained that she would not have much money to pay him back.

"It's okay. Yall come on, get in."

I know, this entire situation seemed like the beginning of a horror movie. The family gets into a car with a stranger and end up dead in a ditch, but what choices did we really have?

We gathered the bare minimum of our things and climbed into the Honda. The man and granny got into the front; my aunt, cousin, brother, and I piled into the back. I was so uncomfortable. I remember thinking this car is no better than ours, we are not going to make it. At some point between my ever-cycling random thoughts, I fell asleep. When I woke, we were exiting the highway into Blueville. As we drove down Wesley street, my granny told the man that she had reached my grandfather and he would give him money for the trouble.

"No, it's okay. If anything, a box of chicken would be nice".

He pulled into CFC. My grandmother offered to buy the biggest bucket they had. He only wanted a two piece. When we arrived home, granny thanked the man for all he had done. He nodded his head in acceptance and drove off. We never saw him again. My granny tried to call him and look him up to repay him later. She never found him. She was convinced he was an angel; still does to this day.

Take them to Church

The church was a significant part of my family growing up. We attended a small church call Temple of Christ. There was the main room, the cafeteria, and two small restrooms. My granny made sure we were in church every Sunday. Sometimes she would even wake us up for Sunday school, a program that took place before the actual praise and worship service. We would be there from 8:00am until 2:00pm. Don't let there be a special program, you will get home at 8:00pm. No wonder we were tired halfway through the pastors preaching. However, you had better not fall asleep. That was a quick way to get popped by granny or pinched by auntie. Wednesdays were Sunshine Band practice days. The choir consisted of four: my cousin Shay, Marq, me & our cousin Octavia. I hated it. I never liked singing in public; I wasn't good at it. I begged my granny to let me out, but she thought it was good for us. "Raise a child in church, and no matter what happens in life, they will always come back," she would say. She told me to just mouthed watermelon whenever I did not want to sing. I did that every youth Sunday.

Whenever I wasn't in school, church, or home, I was at God's love Daycare. It was at a church that ran a daycare during the week. I dreaded going here. The Pastor's daughter was always mean to me. Her name was Veronica. She was tall, skinny, dark, and prissy; I think she was in middle school. Veronica and her siblings basically ran the place. She would always trip me or pushed me. Whenever I told their mom, they would lie about it. The bright side about this place was I met Justine. She was the same age as me, but we went to different schools. We would always play tag whenever they let us go out and play. One day I came in and saw the group of demon seeds surrounding Justine. They called me over.

"Kennadi, come here," yelled Veronica.

I hesitated but went anyway. If I didn't, they would get me later.

"This is Justine," she said.

"I know Justine, we play together," I replied.

"Do you like Justine?"

"Yes, she is my friend."

"I think you like her more than that, say she is your girlfriend."

"No!"

"Say it, or I will tell mom you stole extra cookies yesterday at lunch."

"Ummm." I knew taking extra cookies was wrong, but I really liked them. I stood there trembling, trying not to cry. I looked at Justine, she looked scared. Maybe they told her to do the same thing. I turned and bolted for the restroom. A few seconds later Justine came in.

"You don't have to say it," Justine stated.

I stayed quiet. Oh great, here comes Treasure, Veronica's sister.

"If you say it, she will leave you alone," said Treasure.

"Okay fine!", I said. I left the restroom and returned to the group, "Justine's my girlfriend!"

They all burst into laughter, called me gay and left. What's gay? Never heard that word before. Whatever, the deed was done. I was free, but not for long. Later that day Veronica slapped me. I was wandering the halls, crying when her mom saw me.

"Kennadi what's wrong?" asked Mrs. Winston.

I looked up and saw Darrien, Veronica's brother. I pointed at him.

"What did you do?", she asked him.

I just started crying hysterically until she called my granny to come to get me. I was waiting for my granny in the office. The spawns walked by.

"She blamed you?"

"Yeah," Darrien said.

Veronica laughed, "You didn't do anything."

I waited a little while longer, my granny finally showed up. I explained what happened to my granny, she made sure I never had to go back there again. Instead, I went to the Gee Kingdom. I don't remember much about it, but it was better than God's Love Day Care.

It takes a Village

During the time my mom was gone, people came out of the woodworks. Some came by to help my granny and aunt, some came by to show empathy, others came to be nosey. I started to go out of town more. Often, I would go with my God-mom Tina. Tina was medium height, light skinned, voluptuous woman. She always dressed pretty and loved wearing wedged heels. Tina and my mom had been friends for a long time. She lived next door with her mom and sister. Tina would come by every now and then to check on us and tell me stories about my mom and here when they were younger. Eventually, she moved away to Dallas. She would come by every once in a while and take me out. Sometimes we would go and get ice cream, other times we go to her house. I spent the weekend with her once in her apartment. I think she had to work late one day, so I ended up over her friend's house. She was the prettiest lady I ever saw. She was dark skinned, but her skin seemed to glow with gold specs. She took me outside to play. I chased her around the yard, both of us laughing. It looked like the moonlight was floating around us, it was so dreamy. When I got tired, she picked me up and took me to her home and gave me an orange popsicle.

I am not sure why that moment was so magical. Maybe it was because it was the first time, I was indeed felt happy since my mom left. If I wasn't visiting with me God-mom. I was with my Aunt Diana, she was my mom's half-sister. She lived in a townhouse in Rockwall. I loved her home. It was the first house I remember visiting with stairs. She had two sons; Tae and Dre. Tae was my least favorite. He would be the reason I no longer visited my aunt until he left the house. I was playing in the living room. Tae peeked around the corner.

"Ke, come here," he said.

"Okay," I replied

I stopped coloring and ran into his room. He and his half-brother Cameron were sitting on the bed bottom half of the red metal twin beds they had. Cameron was a year older than me.

"Hey, Cameron," I said.

"Hi" he replied.

"Come over here!", said Tae.

He positioned Cameron and me on the other side of the bunk beds. I was squished there was a little space between the wall and the bed. He told me to lay on the floor. After I laid there, he pulled off my underwear. Then he told Cameron to take off his pants and put him on top of me. We just laid there. I looked under the bed and saw my cousin hanging over the other side of the bed peeking under. He smirked at me, then my aunt busted in.

"Tae where are the kids?", she yelled.

He pointed at us. She came over and found us in the compromising position. She yelled at us to get up. Her and Tae went back and forth. Next thing I know he helps Cameron get dressed and I am being drugged out of the room.

Dre was funny and closer to my age. He took me trick or treating once. It was one street in Blueville that was lined with huge houses. They gave out the king size candy bars. I was dressed as a ghost. I don't think my granny could afford new costumes, so I wore a sheet with two eyes cut out. It was the first time I had been trick or treating. We hopped out of the car to visit a few houses. It wasn't long before my night took a turn for the worse. As I was walking to another house, a little girl in a pink butterfly costume approached me. Well, I am not sure if it was a butterfly or not. It was pink had wings and sparkled everywhere. Maybe it was a fairy. Anyway, she looked at me with her hand on her hip.

"What are you supposed to be?"

I said with pride, "A ghost."

"You're not a ghost, that's just a sheet!"

"I am too a ghost!"

"You're the ugliest ghost I ever saw!"

She then turned and walked away. I felt so crushed, I took off my sheet and threw it on the ground and returned to the van. It took a few minutes for anyone to notice I was missing.

"What's wrong Ke?", Dre asked.

I explained to him what happened.

"Aww Ke, don't let that get to you, you were a great ghost. Come get some candy with me."

"Ummm okay, but I am not wearing that stupid costume."

"Okay, that's fine."

We went back out on the hunt for candy. He saw the little girl who made fun of me.

"Come here Ke lets hide." He was dressed as Freddy Kruger. That face was enough to give me nightmares for weeks. The girl and her friends walked by the bushes we were crouched behind.

"BOO!", screamed Dre.

Ahhhhhhh!

The girls dropped their bags and ran down the street. I laughed so hard. Dre scooped up the bags, and we ran he gave me one bag and kept the other. We dumped the candy into our bags as we walked back to the van.

"Looks like you too had a good run!", said Aunt Diana.

"We did mom," said Dre, as he winked at me.

Occasionally, I would go with my brother to his dad's house. Marvin would come by to bring Marq clothes and shoes, or he would take him out for the day. Sometimes I could go with them. We would go to Blue Lake park where he would chase us around, or we would go to his mom's house and jump on the trampoline. I liked Marvin a lot. I didn't have a dad, it was cool my brother let me share his. One evening Marvin dropped us off at home, my granny wasn't there, so we had to wait in the car. My brother was sleep, and I was bored of waiting.

"Marvin, can I drive?"

"You are too young to drive," he said.

"Aww man."

"I tell you what, you can sit in my lap and turn steer the wheel."

"Okay!"

I climbed over, and he put me on his legs. The car went all the way to the front on the driveway, and all the way back. We did this several times. I honked the horn a few times. Marvin turned up the radio, I drove and sang the songs on the radio. He placed one hand on my thigh, and one hand under his shirt. I could hear him began to hum, maybe he was a shy singer like me. I felt his hand hit my back a few times. After a few songs my brother started to shift, I tried to turn around, but Marvin told me to keep driving.

Eventually, my granny arrived. Marvin put me back in my seat. I noticed the back of my shirt was wet. I guess I had started to sweat. I was sad I couldn't drive anymore, but he told me I could drive some other time again. I was excited. We got out of the car, and he handed Marq to my granny, drove off.

Niya

Niya was coming over today. I could not wait we would play without dolls, dance, watch movies, and play in nail polish. With all the adult people coming in and out of my life at the time I was excited to be with my friend. My granny had a surprise for us. She had set up the swimming pool out back. A car pulled up

"Hey Ke," Niya said as she popped out of the backseat.

"Niya!" I ran to the car to help her get her stuff. She said bye to her mom, then can into change for the pool. She was wearing a flowery pink one piece. I wore my red and white two-piece. We walked back to the porch striking a pose back to back. Ms. Adrienne burst out laughing.

"Get it y'all," said granny.

We hoped in the pool. We played Polo Marco and tried to see who could go underwater the longest. After about an hour our feet started to get pruney, not to mention the mosquitos started eating us alive. Those stupid off candles were not working. We got out and ran to the back door. Granny met us and gave a towel. She had already run a bath for Niya and told me to get her a wash off towel. We went to the restroom. I reached in the top cabinet to get the towel.

"Thanks," she said.

"Welcome," I replied.

"Hey, give me your hand," she said. She tried to put it between her legs.

"I'm not touching that!"

"Just do it."

I hesitated but did it anyway. She burst out laughing, and I got out of there. I took a shower, I hated baths. All I thought about was people feet being where my butt was. Gross, the thought made me shiver. After dinner, it was almost time for bed. Granny put us in bed and let us watch one episode of the Power Girls.

"I'm the red one," she shouted.

"I'm bubble cup!"

No one wanted to be bubbles she cried way too much. We pretended to fight bad guys until it was time to sleep. Granny came back and cut the tv off thirty minutes later. We tossed and turned and tried to get comfortable. I decided to lay on my side so did Niya. I was starting to doze until Niya began rubbing herself against me. I scooted backward. A few minutes later she did it again. I laid trying to figure out what she was doing. Then she rolled over and kissed me. I didn't move, and she kissed me again. I didn't fight it, plus I had been in this situation before.

My aunt Tiff lived in some apartments briefly. Whenever I went over, I would play with this girl named Abby. She was a tall, thin girl with a short haircut. If not for her name, you would think she was a boy. We would sit out in the courtyard and make mud pies. She invited me to come to play at her house and to eat. Her mom was making tacos. My aunt said it was okay, so we ran to her apartment. She showed me her room which was loaded with toys. She had a vanity and everything. We immediately started playing dress up. She only had one fancy dress, so I just played with the jewelry.

"Hey, you want to go in my mom's closet? She has a lot of dresses."

"YEAH!"

We went into her moms' closet. I was trying on shoes when Abby hit the lights. I turned to see what was going on.

"Abby?"

She was standing right in front of me.

"What are you---"

She pulled me down to the floor, climbed on top of me, and kissed me. I pulled back and pushed her. I ran out of the closet and out of the front door. I walked back to my aunt's house and didn't mention it ever. Shortly after that, my aunt moved back with my granny. I never saw Abby again.

With Niya, this would happen each time she came over after that. It didn't stop until we got caught at school. We were in the second grade then; different classes. She saw me in the hallway, leaving the bathroom and we kissed.

"Ohhhhhh, I am telling," said Terry, our classmate.

I pulled back turned and ran back to class. I hoped no one would believe him, but after that, I kept my distance. No more sleepovers for me I thought.

Tragedy Strikes Again

The next time I saw my mom, I was with PaPa, my grandpa. My granny and aunt had to work on that visiting day; Shay and Marq were with their dads. I loved road trips with my grandpa. We always stopped to eat both going to see mom and coming back. We would cruise down the road listening to Tootsy Collins and Johnny Tailored, the oldies. My favorite song was by, Wayne Kenne, B & A Conversation. We would sing that song at the top of our lungs. When we weren't singing, I was enjoying the view of the country fields of various farm animals, or asleep in the back. PaPa had a bed in the back of his van. Mom looked different this time, her hair was longer. I ran up to her and squeezed her legs. She kissed my forehead and held my hand as we walked to the table. This time I was able to color while her and my grandpa talked. A siren went off.

"What's going on?", PaPa asked.

"That's the alarm for lockdown."

"It's not going to affect our time is it?"

"It might."

A guard rushed over and took my mom back. Another escorted us out of the facility. Turns out there was a stabbing, and the prison was on lockdown. I was so angry, I cried most of the way home. Well at least until we stopped a Briggs's for ice cream. PaPa got me the biggest mint chocolate chip ice cream cone I had ever eaten.

When I arrived home, Aunt Tiff was sitting on the porch. My grandpa hoped out the car to talk to her as I went into the house. If I had learned anything at that point, it was to stay out of grown folks' business. That would usually get you a whopping quick.

The next morning was the weekend. Thank goodness no school. First grade was fun, but the second grade was hard. We had to study hard for some state test, STAKS. I woke up and made some cinnamon toast crunch then planted myself on the couch in front of the tv. Ed, Edda, and Eddi a marathon was on, I always wanted one of those Tooth Breakers. I guess I fell asleep when my aunt woke up, she was running through the house holding my brother's hand and holding the phone. It took a while to notice, but my brother was bleeding. His thumb had been sliced in half, the top part was dangling off the side off. My eyes were wide, my aunt was in full panic mode. Uncle Steve, Shay's dad, walked through the door.

"What happened?", he asked.

"His thumb, I walked in the kitchen, and it was just hanging off," she replied.

"What happened little man?", Steve asked my brother.

"I tried to cut the skin off my apple."

"You can't do that, you are too young to use a knife."

He calmed my aunt and packed us in the car to head to the hospital. My brother had to get stitches to hold his thumb in place. Later that night my aunt and Steve went out to a party. My granny got off late, so my aunt ended up meeting Steve there. Granny walked in, and Tiff walked out. She was gone for two minutes it seemed before she stumbled back in sobbing. She ran to her room and changed clothes.

"Tiff what's wrong?", I asked my granny.

"Steve was in an accident, the party got shut down early by the police as he was headed home, he turned a corner to fast and slammed into a building wall. I'm going to the scene now", my aunt said.

"Tiff---"

"Mom I will be back I can't talk now, said my aunt as she dashed out the door."

Granny let us stay up late that night. A few hours later she returned home. Tiff came in and just folded over onto my granny. Uncle Steve had passed. He was pinned in between the wall and smushed inside his car. Rescuers didn't cut him out in time, and he didn't make it. The energy around was sober for weeks. Between balancing work, preparing to bury the love of her life, and consoling her daughter she was a mess. My granny was no better. Tragedy had struck again; two fatherless children now shared the same roof.

Caterpillar

Fourth grade was starting, it had changed this year. We no longer sat in one classroom all day. We now rotated to different classes for each subject., but we still had a homeroom where we spent most of the day. I walked in the class, I spotted Jazelle and rushed over. Jazelle was Shay's older cousin. We met at the funeral over the summer.

"Hey, Zelle."

"What's up Ke," she said as we sat down in our desk next to each other.

"Nothing everything good, I like your shoes."

"Thanks, I like your hair, how's Shay?"

"She is holding up, how's your grandma?"

"She not doing too well."

I said nothing, just made a sympathetic face. I was no good at speaking about death. As everyone piled into class, I saw another face I recognized. Tiana Jordan. She was in my class last year.

"Hey girl!" I shouted she came over. I introduced them.

"Zelle this Tiana, she was in my class last year."

The class was starting, so we had to end the conversation there. We went with the day as usual different subjects, changing classes, and lunch. Finally, it was time for recess. At this time all the fourth graders went out together. Zelle, Tiana, and I posted up on a bench and talked and laughed. Suddenly, this group of girls approached us. Joy, Kendra, Niya, and Amber, they were supposed to be the popular girls at the school.

"Hey Ke," said Niya.

I just looked at her.

Joy said, "You don't have to speak to her."

"First of all, what that got to do with you?" Zelle said

"I wasn't talking to you," Joy responded and rolled her neck.

(Smack) The sound of Tiana punching her in the face. Zelle and I jumped up. Amber, Tiana's cousin, grabbed Tiana. Next thing I know it was a full-on brawl. Zelle pulling Amber hair, Tiana sitting on Joy punching her face. I had Niya in a headlock when Kendra jumped on my back. A circle formed around us. This went on for about five minutes before the teachers broke it up. All of us were sent to the office. Joy and Kendra got licks by the principal; the rest of us were sent to in-school suspension (ISS). Zelle, Tiana and I passed notes back and forth discussing what just happened and calling them shokes. We were thick as thieves from that day on. School was over, and I was happy the school day was over. I was not built for ISS. That all changed when I got to the car.

"So, you were fighting at school huh?"

"Niya started---"

"I don't wanna hear it! Just wait 'til we get home. Got people calling my job." Granny was steamed. I started crying. "Crying won't save you now, when we get home gone pick your switch," she said.

We arrived home, I went ahead and picked the smallest switch I could find. Boy that was a mistake, it seemed like the smaller the switch, the worse the sting. From then on, I swore to never get into any fights at school, my butt could not handle it.

A couple of weeks had passed, Mrs. Martin had informed me that I did exceptionally well on the practice test, and she was recommending me for the talented and gifted (TAG) program. TAG was a program that took place once a week at a different school. We would take the bus to the other school and participate in advanced studies. I was worried I would be alone, but I found out my cousin made it as well; her name was Zaria. She was Kendra's half-sister. No worries though, she was chill, nothing like her sister, to be honest, I don't even think they liked each other. I could understand that. I had a half-sister myself. We never really saw each other except for pop up visits at my grandma Jean's house. Jean was my dad's mom. I would visit her sometimes on the weekends. My sister name was Kaydence, we played well together at grandma, but we never talked outside of her place.

Zaria and I bonded on the trips to the new school. We were the only two black kids in the entire program. There was one girl named Misha who was half black. She didn't go to our school, but at TAG we always hung out. She would tell us about her school, and we would speak about ours. TAG was different from our regular school. We learned about history, the arts, algebra, and put on plays. Zaria and I even built the Globe Theatre out of sugar clubs and popsicle sticks. TAG was all fun, there was no set schedule, things were different each time we went. However, I couldn't help but feel like I was missing out, I missed Zelle and Tiana.

Not to worry though they would always update me on what was going on. Like the time we got a new student in the class. His name was Tristian, all the girls were fawning all over this guy; especially my girl Zelle. He was tall, dark, and fine, at least to them. I didn't see it, but I tried to hook them up once. We wrote a letter asking him to go with Zelle. It had bears, glitter, and perfume; sadly, that letter was smeared in the process of giving it to him, years later we found out he never read it. Tiana had an on and off boyfriend. Every time they broke up, I remember her crying in the back storage by the backpacks.

I had a crush on an older boy named Tyreke. He was one of my classmate's older brothers. Light skinned, fine, with freckles. His eyes were gray, and he was taller than me which was rare. Since kindergarten, I always towered over everyone. He was a grade above me, they got out of school earlier. I saw him all the time at recess, it was right before school was out. He would meet me at the fence, and we would just talk about everything; you know cartoons and stuff. Until he stopped coming, then I noticed Thomas wasn't there either; it turns out they had moved. Well at least after that I focused more on school work, on the final TAKS test I passed reading and math with a perfect score. There was an awards ceremony, and I got a trophy. My granny was smiling from ear to ear, and my aunt was crying.

The next major event would be Zelle's epic birthday party. Her mom rented a limo, I had never been in a limo before. Mrs. Janet had arranged for the limo to pick all the girls up from school. This was all good and fun until I realized it wouldn't be just Zelle, Tiana, and I. All her cousins would be there. Zelle had a big family, most of her cousins were older except one. Her name was Breontay, she was from Dallas. She rarely smiled, her mug stayed on, and she was quick to speak her mind. I was convinced she hated me. She was Zelle best cousin, I was Zelle best friend. I was not comfortable in this situation; I kept my distance. Tiana and I hung out most of the ride. We bonded with Zelle's little cousin. We were driven to the mall, Si Si's for dinners, and then back to Zelle's grandmas for a sleepover. The day was terrific, but that night Zelle was over it. Zelle wanted to dance and have a pillow fight; the older girls wanted to tell ghost stories and play light as a feather, stiff as a board.

Some game where you lifted someone in the air with two fingers. Zelle got upset and went into the den. Tiana and I followed her.

"Are you okay?"

"No, I don't want to play that mess. It's my birthday."

"Well let's mess it up," Tiana said.

"How?" I asked.

"Well, they are playing in the dark."

"So..."

"Let's throw hangers at them. They won't know what it is."

"Okay," I said

Zelle nodded in agreement. We threw hangers each time they started saying that stupid chant.

"Who throwing stuff?", someone said.

"Ouch," another groaned.

We kept throwing until we heard a scream. The lights came on. Zelle's older cousin's nose was bleeding. Seems like a hanger had popped her in the face. The adults were outside at the time, one of Zelle's cousin went to go tell. Mrs. Janet came in fuming.

"Who was throwing?", asked Mrs. Janet.

No one said a word.

"Oh, yall can't speak now, well everybody goes to bed."

Zelle Tiana and I slept in Zelle's grandmas' room, we whispered and talked all night. Finally sleeping after the sun rose the next day. Over the summer Zelle, Tiana, and I spoke on the phone a lot. We rarely saw each other though.

If I wasn't home, I was on the road visiting my mother. Zelle spent the summer in Dallas with her cousins and Tiana spent the summer visiting her sister in California.

Nevaeh

Towards the end of the summer, Zelle came back to Blueville. She asked me if I wanted to come spend the night. I was definitely in. When I got there, she was sitting on the couch, Nevaeh was there too. I greeted them as I put my bags on the couch. They each took turns talking about their summers. I told them I was home most of the time, because I hadn't told anyone about my mom and dad's situation, and I didn't plan to either. We watched movies and made up dance routines. For dinner we ate burritos courtesy of Mrs. Janet, them things were too good. Mrs. Janet let us drink a soda that night. After that, we all were as good as dead. We all put on our pajamas and crashed. If you don't know, a full belly puts me to sleep quick.

School was about to start. Everyone was going shopping and getting ready to look fly on their first day. After all, we would no longer be in elementary school, we were moving on up. Next year all fourth graders from all the elementary schools would come together and make up the fifth grade. I was excited and scared at the same time, but those feelings didn't last long.

"Ke," called my granny.

"Yes?"

"I need to talk to you," Granny said.

"Okay, are we going shopping today?"

"No not today."

"Okay." I waited for her to speak.

"Sit down, I need to tell you something."

I became worried. "What's wrong?" The only time my granny hesitated to speak was when she was giving me bad news.

"Nevaeh Johnson passed."

"Who?"

"Nevaeh."

I swear my heart fell out of my chest and hit the floor. "What, How? Are you sure it's her?", I started to weep. "I just saw her," I cried.

"I know," my granny wrapped her arms around me.

I was shaking and crying, I didn't care about school anymore. I didn't care about anything. I wanted to know why God kept allowing those around me to die. I just met her. I didn't understand.

"What happened?"

"She was at the city pool, she got on the water slide and bumped her head at the bottom. She was unconscious."

"Why didn't anybody help? I said with tears rolling down my face?"

"It was crowded, no one saw her. She was found an hour later when her body floated up in the six-foot section of the pool."

This made me cry harder. All those people there and no one thought to help her. I was so angry. I ran into the room and threw myself on the bed. I laid there crying thinking about all the fun we had just had together. I hated my life. All I could think was why. Oh crap, Zelle. I called Zelle's home ten times, no one answered. I understood. She would reach out to me when she could. Later the next day she called.

"Ke, Zelle on the phone," said, granny

"He-Hello" I stuttered.

"Hey she," said somberly.

"How are you?"

"I can't believe it. We just saw her. All I can think about is Nevaeh".

I didn't say anything I just nodded, not that she could see me."Do you want to talk about it?"

"No, I want to remember the good times."

"Okay," I said, I started talking to her about the dance routine we all made up. I care by Caliyah. We barely made it through the chorus without bursting into tears. "I'm so sorry."

The line went silent, then I heard sobbing.

"Kennadi, Zelle is going to call you back later," Mrs. Janet said.

"Yes Mam," I said before I hung up.

A week had passed before the funeral. I didn't go. I couldn't go. I didn't want to see another dead body again in my life. My aunt went through, she said it was sad, but Nevaeh looked peaceful. She wore a sparkling red princess dress and was surrounded by all her favorite dolls. I remember riding around with my granny that day while she took care of errands. I just sat in the car and looked out the window, there was nothing that could change the way I was feeling that day. Nevaeh was gone.

The Return

I was still struggling with what had happened over the summer. I held sadness in my mind and anger in my heart. The only thing I remember is some stupid boy in one of my classes kept calling me a tree because of my height. I didn't respond so he kept going. He talked about my shoes and my hair. I was still unbothered until he then said something about my father. How dare he? He didn't know my father or me. I calmly stood up, walked up to him and grabbed him by his neck. I held him in the air for what seemed like a minute. I slowly turned my head to look at my teacher. She just stood there wide-eyed. She looked like she was stuck between heading for the door and coming to help. I looked terrible at the scrawny boy and gently put him back down. Then I sat in my seat as nothing happened. I knew there would be consequences, but I just didn't care. Over the summer before sixth grade, my mom was set to be released from prison. This was it, the one thing I needed to get me out of the mood I had been in, the cure to my anger.

It seemed like it the last few weeks dragged, but it didn't matter, because today was the day. My brother and I could not contain our excitement. We were going to meet mom at Aunt Diana's house. It was about noon when we all got in the car and headed to Aunt Diana's house. When we arrived, there were balloons everywhere and a welcome home banner across the walkway. Shay, Marq and I played with balloons as we waited. What seemed like hours later, my mom walked in. We ran to her. We were now tall enough now to grab her waist. She wrapped her arms around us and cried.

Everyone else stood around clapping, taking pictures, and whipping tears from their eyes. As everyone calmed down, she walked in the kitchen and made us plates. We ate and watched cartoons while the adults talked and danced. This house was filled with pure bliss. As the day came to an end, my brother and I would have to leave. I did not understand, you mean to tell me I waited eight years to see my mother and now I must leave her again. Apparently, her old friends wanted to take her out that day and have an adult sleepover. I didn't give a crap about any of that. I got my shoes, and got in the car, my brother did as well. Funny thing is, he didn't even cry this time, it was like he just did not care.

The ride back to granny's was quiet. My aunt had stayed to party with mom, so it was just granny and us kids. We got out of the car and went into the house. I laid on my bed still fuming. I just could not believe this. I hardly slept that night. I tossed and turned as anger took over my mind. The next morning, I woke up to an argument.

"Why doesn't she want to stay here?", granny asked.

"You know why," aunt Tiff said.

"I thought she would be over it by now her kids live here."

"Well, I guess she is not."

I crept closer to the kitchen where they were arguing. I walked on my tippy toes so I could not be detected. Over what I thought?

"It happened over ten years now. I don't understand, the kids live here, we live here, is she too good now? "

"No mom, it just affected her differently, I don't think she should come back to where it happened."

"Okay Tiff, I will let this one go," said Granny, "Where is she going to stay?"

"With daddy," Tiff said.

What?!? How messed up it that. My father killed by my mother, now she doesn't want to live with us, and I have

47

"She still wears pigtails," Tisha replied.

"A big ass baby," Tawnya said.

The rest of them just laughed. They were talking about me. My granny did her best to fix our hair; however, I think she could not create age-appropriate hairstyles for me. Zelle rolled her eyes.

"Ke, your hair is fine," Zelle assured me.

Tiana stood up to head over, but I grabbed her arm and told her not to worry about it. Darnell was walking up to the table at the time.

"Shut up Monique you just mad she ain't bald headed like you," he said.

He sat down with the guys at the table with Braylon, Dekorian, Oliver, and Juan, the popular guys. After we ate breakfast, Zelle came with me to the bathroom to help me take down my hair. I brushed it up into a ponytail. She gave me a hug, and we went our separate ways.

My first class of the day was English, next was science/ social studies, then math. Math was my favorite class. It was the only time I didn't feel alone. A class I shared with Mr. Stevenson himself and Braylon. Braylon was annoying at school, but when he wasn't with his crew, he was cool. He sometimes came by my granny house on the weekend, and we would just talk. Mrs. Taylor was our math teacher. She split her classroom in half, girls on one side boys on the other. I sat directly across from Darnell. The rest of the day was good until PE. I ended up having PE with the same girls from breakfast. Just my luck. Since it was the first day of school, the PE instructors let us choose the activity for the day. The vote was to play dodgeball. It was all fun and games until…. (CLAP). The sound of the ball smacking Tisha in the face. I tried to play it off like I didn't know what happened. I had already had a run in with these girls. I was not looking to deal with them again.

"Who threw that?", Tisha screamed.

My teammates looked at each other.

"It was Kennadi ugly self," Monique said.

I looked at Tisha. She picked up a ball and headed towards me. My mind said run, but my body would not move. She slammed the ball into my head three times and pushed me. I pushed her back, but then her friends surrounded me. Coach blew her whistle.

"That is enough. Go change and get ready for school dismissal", she said. Everyone went into the locker room to get dressed except me. Coach thought it was best me and Tisha wasn't in the dressing room at the same time. Tisha came out, and I went in. As I was getting dressed, I heard someone approach me.

"Sorry that happened you."

I looked up, it was Trina Kinley. I knew her from last year. People made fun of her because a roach crawled out of her backpack once. I didn't, trust me I knew what it was like to live with roaches. Overnight it seemed they would crowd the kitchen floor. If I wanted water, I would literally skip through them to get to the fridge. My granny would sometimes bomb the house with bug killer, but they would always come back.

"I'm okay."

"They get on my nerves, they always got something to say," she replied.

I just nodded. I didn't feel like discussing what just happened. I just wanted to get dressed and go home. On the bus ride, Zelle told me about what she and Tiana did, and about the boy she liked in her class named T.J., I waved to Zelle as I got off the bus. As I walked into the house, my mom granny and aunt were sitting on the couch. Marq was in my room

"Sup Ke?", Marq said.

"What you doing here? You not supposed to get out of school yet."

"I got kicked out of school today."

"Why?', I asked.

"I got in trouble. Jake gave me some weed to hold for him. I wasn't going to smoke it, but the teacher found it in my backpack."

"What? Did you tell them that?"

"Yeah, he got kicked out too. We gotta go to BAEP."

BAEP used to be Johnston elementary. They turned it into an alternative school for those that got in trouble a lot or didn't focus well in the regular school classroom.

"There's more, momma, here."

"I saw her."

"Yeah, they in there talking about us moving out with her."

"What, I ain't going!

"Ke, we should go she our mom."

"Well, she has been back a while now she doesn't want us."

"Yes she does, she just had to get herself together."

"Whatever."

Marq sat on my bed and watched tv as I started on my homework. I don't know about him by I was okay living with my grandmother. Her and my aunt have always been there for us, and I just didn't see my mom and me ever getting along. I just had too much rage for her. Not only did she kill my father, but I felt like she killed herself right along with him. I was left, I felt like an orphan. Later, that night after my mother left, my granny sat us down to let us know that my mom would be moving in with us tomorrow, she wanted to come home and be with her children. I accepted this news. At least I wouldn't have to leave my granny.

The Attack

My mom moved back in things, and things seemed tense.
Everyone was walking on eggshells. My aunt and grandma
were not at home as much. My mom had started a job at
Subline, but she was at home when we got home from
school. I would come in and go straight to my room. I made
sure there was little opportunity for us to communicate.
Soon I would be forced to interact with her tough.

After school as I approached the back door. I had left my
key at home, and my granny always left a spare hidden
under a rock on the back porch. I was about to walk in
when I heard the adults talking.

"Mom, you have to let go, they are her kids," Tiff
exclaimed.

"I promise I will take care of them," my mom said.

"I had them most of their lives," granny cried.

"I know that, and I am grateful, I just want the opportunity
to bond with my kids, I can't do that here."

There was a long silence, "Okay we can tell them today,"
she said with a scratchy voice.

I turned and walked from that door and the house. I ran
over to my God moms. I explained to her what just
happened. She explained to me that I should give my
mother a chance to start over. She was right. I couldn't hate
my mother forever, mainly because I didn't even really
know what happened, I had heard so many stories. It was
an accident, it was planned, my mother was jealous, my
dad was abusive. There was even more drama, one guy
who thought he was my father would show up at my
granny's house and my school. He always commented that
I looked like him. I was sick of it. Maybe one way to move

on was to reconnect with my mother, and when our bond was stronger, perhaps she would tell me what happened. We moved into this yellow house in the Heights. I don't know why it was called heights. To me, it seemed like the lowest area in Blueville. It was a small three-bedroom house.

My room was so small if I opened the door it hit my bed, but it was okay we lived ten minutes from my grandmother's house. My brother was excited because he finally had his own room. My mom made tacos for dinner that night and deemed all Tuesdays going forward Taco Tuesday. After dinner, we played board games. I enjoyed laughing at my mom and brother play twester. This was only the first night, but things were going well. There was a knock on the door, my mom paused the game to go answer it. It was my brother's father, Marvin. This guy had not been around in a few years. He always told my brother he would come to get him but left him waiting on the porch all day with tears streaming down his face. Last time I saw him, he showed up at my brother's football game drunk. He embarrassed my brother and ranted about how my brother was terrible. Marq ran off the field crying, it was his first year playing. He quit at the next team practice. My granny confronted his dad. She told him if he came near us again, she would kick his funky ass and have him arrested. That was followed up by my grandfather's death threat. To my surprise, my mom let him in. He gave her a hug as he came in the door, I remember wincing at him grabbing her butt. I looked over to see how my little brother was reacting, he had already left and gone to his room, I did the same. Looking at this man would only add fuel to my inner rage. I watched Pick at night until I fell asleep. I woke up to the sound of my mom singing. I rolled over and looked at the clock, it was 1am. Marvin was still there, I could hear his deep voice through the walls. I had a field trip the next day, so I just rolled over, placed a pillow over my face, and went back to sleep.

The next morning my mom woke us up for breakfast, she had made us pancakes. I had on my favorite B- Unit shirt and some khaki cargo pants.

"Ke, why don't you wear that purple dress I bought you?"

"We are going to a museum ma, I don't need to wear a dress."

"I think you should always look your best," mom explained.

"I do ma."

"Okay, baby."

I ate breakfast and hurried off to the bus stop. The bus ride to school was different because I got picked up outside my new house. Luckily, I was still allowed to ride the same bus.

"Girl, I got something to tell you," Zelle said.

"What's up?"

"Are you ready?

"What is it?"

"Zaria and Darnell are going out."

"What?!?"

She continued talking, but I heard nothing. I was inside my own head. I was crushed. My thought ran through my head why her? Forget both, I hate them. We finally arrived at school. As we headed to class, I saw Darnell in the hall.

"What's up Kennadi?"

I ignored him looked up and kept walking

"Hey, you don't hear me?", he asked.

"I heard you, I don't have anything to say."

"What did I do?"

I turned to walk away, he grabbed my arm. (Smack) The sound of my hand going across his face he stood there in shock, as I slammed my locker and walked away. In class before the field trip, our teacher told us that we were required to stay with our homeroom teacher the entire time, great! The bus ride to the museum was so long. Science Places, it had so many exhibits. There were planetary exhibits, an aquarium, and an exhibit related to dinosaurs. My favorite one was a medical exhibit. There was a giant robotic hand that you could operate, and a body laid on a table with a tv recording showing a doctor giving heart surgery. For lunch we had a picnic on the museum lawn when we were done, we were able to play on this purple octopus looking path that spread out over the pond. This was one of the best field trips I ever went on. We returned to school thirty minutes before school was to be dismissed. We had to return to our homeroom classrooms until dismissal. (Pssst) I looked up. Darnell threw a note over.

Why are you mad at me? The note said. I threw the note back. Our teacher saw it, Darnell ripped a sheet of paper out of his notebook and gave it to her. It had math notes on it, so she didn't make a scene. After she looked it over and walked away, he read the real note. *I can't talk to you anymore*, I had replied. He looked at me and mouthed why not? The bell rang, and we were dismissed. I got up and walked out. On the bus ride home. Zelle told me how she kissed her crush during the planetary showing, while I told her I slapped mine. I got off the bus at my granny house.

This way I wouldn't be on the bus alone. As I was walking to my granny's, I saw my grandfather at the store.

"Ke-Baby!"

I gave him a hug and wrapped my arm around his waist. "Can you take me home?"

"Sure!"

He bought me some snacks, and we headed off.

"How was school today?"

"I slapped someone."

"With them rough hands, you probably slapped the skin off his face."

I burst out laughed, "I sure tried."

We both burst out laughing until we arrived at the house.

"Alright Ke!"

"Bye PaPa."

I turned the key to open the door. To my surprise, Marvin was sitting on the couch.

"What's up Ke?", He said slurred, he had been drinking. If his voice wasn't a giveaway, his red eyes and the smell gave it away.

"Hi," I said as I anxiously headed to my room. I threw my backpack on the bed and turned to shut the door. Marvin pushed it back open.

"What is it?", I said.

"You look good today," he said.

After the conversation I had with my mom that morning, I knew that was a lie. I tried to shut the door again, this time he pushed his way in. He then pushed me on to my bed. I screamed and tried to fight him off. He punched me in the face. I screamed again as loud as I could, it seemed he hit me as hard as he could. My body froze, and my head was pounding. Everything started happening in slow motion, I could feel blood dripping down my face. I started drifting in and out of consciousness. The last thing I saw was Marvin standing over me.

I woke up, my clock said 6:35pm. I rolled out of bed and went to the restroom. As I walked, I felt sore, and my head was pounding. I sat down to pee, and my privates burned, I looked down, and there was blood in my underwear. I cleaned myself up and headed to the kitchen. I could smell food, my mom had to be cooking.

"Mom I think…. I looked over and saw Marvin still sitting on the couch. Mom, I think I started my period", I said. We had learned about periods in a puberty presentation last year.

"What happened to your face?"

"I got into a fight I said."

Marvin smirked.

"With who? The school didn't tell---"

"It wasn't that serious ma."

"Okay, did you win?"

"Do you have any pads?", I whispered trying to change the topic.

"Oh yeah. Oh my God, my baby is becoming a woman. When I get back, we are taking a picture."

My mom always took pictures of every moment. My mom went to get the pads, I grabbed the biggest knife from the kitchen drawer and ran to my room. I tucked it at the edge of the bed right under the top mattress. If Marvin ever came for me again, I would kill him. My mom knocked on the door and gave me the pads, she then went to finish dinner. I wanted to tell my mom that Marvin had hit me, but to be honest, I was scared. Maybe it was my fault. I was taught never to disrespect an adult. Maybe I disrespected him by shutting the door in his face. I returned to the living room, Marvin was gone. After I showered, applied a pad, took some Advil, and went to sleep. The next morning, I asked to stay home, I knew Marvin had work, and I wasn't worried. Plus, I had my knife. I told her I wasn't feeling well from starting my period. I was still bleeding, and my head hurt. She gave me the okay and hugged me on her way out. I took a few more pills and went back to bed. I must have been tired because I didn't wake up until about 3:00pm. I went to the kitchen made me a sandwich and grabbed a bag of hot Heetos. The doorbell rang, I grabbed the first knife I saw. I walked over to the peephole. I put the knife down.

"Darnell? What are you doing here?"

"I noticed you missed school, after yesterday I wanted to see if you were okay. What happened to your head?"

Oh, crap I thought I look a mess. I was still in my pajamas with a hole in the knee. My hair was in a sad side ponytail. My face was still swollen from the hit. "I will be back. Meet me in the back."

I ran to the room to change, I put on jeans and my yellow butterfly shirt. Then I quickly brushed my hair into a ponytail and headed to the backyard. We sat on the trampoline.

"How was school?", I asked.

"It was fine. In homeroom, Braylon showed Mrs. Taylor what the p pop was. She freaked out. Why did you miss school?"

"I wasn't feeling well."

"Does it have anything to do with the knot on your head?"

"Yeah, I ran into a wall."

"I know you not that clumsy."

"I---I---," I burst into tears. I couldn't lie, I needed to talk to someone. I told him what had happened the day before. I sobbed most of the time, but I think he got the point. He put his arm around my shoulders and let me cry until I got myself together. We sat there in silence for a while. He then told me that his dad was beating him. He at least got beaten once a week for the past year. He then raised his shirt to show me the scars on his back. I would never have known. More silence. I didn't know what to say. He decided to change the topic.

"Why did you slap me yesterday?", he asked.

There was no way I was telling him I cared about him, I may have been jealous of my cousin, but I still wouldn't betray her like that. "I was just having a bad day, I am sorry."

"It's okay, but next time you have a bad day, let me know."

"Ke.... Kennadi!" It was my mom, I didn't even hear her car pull up. Darnell and I walked to the front.

"Hey Ms. Kassie," Darnell said.

"How do you know my mom?", I asked.

"His mother and I work together," she answered.

"I'm going to head home," he said.

"See you at school," I said

"We don't have school tomorrow."

"Oh, okay well see you later."

"Tell your mom I said hello," my mom yelled.

"Yes mam," he said as he turned and walked down the street.

"What was he doing here?"

"He came to see why I wasn't in school."

"Umm hum," she said with a smile.

(Ring)

"What?!? I'm on my way!"

"We have to go pick up Marq, Marvin didn't show," she said.

 On the way my mom repeatedly called Marvin, he didn't answer. She left messages on his voicemail cursing him out. When we arrived at the school, my mom ran in to get my brother. I saw her talking with the teacher, and I assumed she was explaining what happened. Later that night Marvin came by. My mom would not let him in. He banged and kicked the door, then my mom called the police. They arrived and arrested Marvin. That was it, he and my mom were over. She tried to hold it together, but I could hear her crying through the wall.

At church, as people were coming in, I saw Darnell and his family. I guess my mom invited them. That Sunday in church my mom went down to the altar for prayer. She cried, and my granny shouted. It was a moving service.

After bonding over out stepdads, Darnell and I grew closer. We talked after church, and instead of sting with Zelle on the bus, I would sit with him. After a few days, Zelle confronted me.

"So, you finally start talking to him, and you don't need me anymore," she yelled.

"It's not like that, we just bonded over something."

"What?"

"It's personal."

"So, you are keeping secrets now. Fine, you're not my best friend anymore."

"Zelle, Hello? Hellooo?"

She hung up on me.

The next morning at school Zaria approached me.

"Why are you sitting next to my boyfriend on the bus?", she asked.

"What?" Oh crap, Zelle must have told, "we just be talking."

"Yeah whatever everyone knows you like him."

Did everyone know I wondered? "Girl get out of my face."

(Pop)

She punched me in the face, then her half-sister Kendra pushed me onto the ground. I tried to get up then Zaria kicked me. They jumped me. Mrs. Frida broke up the fight, and we all went to the office. They got suspended. I went to

ISS for the day but was free to go. That was the last time I rode the bus. From then on, my aunt, granny, and mom took turns taking me to school. I avoided Darnell at school and kept my head down. I would see Tiana, Zelle, and Amber hanging out, but I avoided them as well. I would only talk to Tiana on the phone.

The God-Family

Over the summer I asked my mom if I could spend the summer with my God-mom. With all the drama going on, I just wanted to escape. My God-mom had moved to Irving, Texas. I had never even heard of it before, but it was about thirty minutes from Dallas. It was a lot busier than Blueville. I couldn't spend the entire month with her, but I could stay for a weekend. The day had come, and Tina was coming to get me.

"You ready to go?", mom asked.

"Yes ma, I need a little break," I said.

"I understand," she replied, "Tina should be 10 minutes away, go make sure you have everything!"

I went to my room and checked my bags to make sure I had everything. I heard the horn outside and headed out the door. "Bye Ma"

"Wait!" She ran up to give me a hug, a kiss and gave me some extra money in case I wanted to buy something.

"Bye baby, have fun."

As I approached the car, I noticed it was full. All I was thinking was who these people are? My god mom introduced me to everyone. Alicia was my god-mom's roommate. She was tall and had long wavy hair, she reminded me of my sister. Neisha was Alicia's little cousin. She was younger than me but way taller. Peter was Alicia's light-skinned nephew. Dajia was Alicia's god-daughter. I spoke, but I was uncomfortable. I hated meeting new people.

The car was packed so I sat in the trunk on the way there. Honestly, I didn't mind, I needed some time to myself anyway. The first night was laid back we all got comfortable being around each other and introducing ourselves, mostly me. Turns out Dajia and I were in the same grade and went to the same school. My god-mom had bought video games for us to play. We spent the entire night alternating the games Def Jam Fight for New Jersey and Mario's Mansion on game cube until we dozed. This was the most fun I had had in a long time.

"Girl last night you scared us," Dajia said.

"How?", I asked.

"You fell asleep on the couch. We tried to wake you, so you could get in the bed., but as soon as we touched you, your eyes opened they were bloodshot red."

I giggled, "I must have been tired."

"Hey y'all get dressed, we are going out today," Alicia said.

We all got dressed and headed out. We headed to Irving Mall. I was like a kid in a candy store, it was way bigger than our little mall in Blueville. I bought shoes, a spray-painted hoodie, and some M&N cookies, they were so soft, my favorite. I would always get them at town east mall when we went school shopping with my mom. For dinner, we went to Chompo's. Chompo's was a Tex-Mex buffet restaurant. Their chimichangas were to die for. After this, we went back to the house and played the game again until we crashed. Today was the time to go home, however, because we all got along, we would do this at least once a month. Each time we went to visit it was a new adventure. We would go to amusement parks, cabins, and concerts. These trips helped pass the time.

After I returned home, a surprise would be waiting for me.

"Ke?"

"Huh?", I said rubbing the sleep from my eyes.

"Girl, wake your ass up!"

I knew that voice, I wiped my beady eyes and opened them wide. "Kabrian?!? What are you doing here?"

Kabrian, known as KD was my "cousin" from Houston. I am not sure if we were truly related, or he was called my cousin due to our parent's friendship. He lived here with his dad a while ago until. His dad went to jail. Now he was living with his grandmother. Turns out he had moved back to Blueville. I gave him a hug. We caught up with each other.

(Ring)

There was someone at the door. It was Niya and her mom. Mrs. Adrienne used to date my Uncle Keith. They came over to see Kabrian. Niya and I were not speaking, but it didn't stop the excitement that filled the room. Later we all took a walk around the neighborhood and ended up at my granny's house. Where we said our goodbyes. However, I would see him on Sunday. Our grandmothers went to church together.

Before church, I was sitting down talking to Darnell.

"Boy get away from her," Kabrian yelled.

Darnell looked up confused.

"He just my friend," I replied

"Nope, I said get away from her."

"I will see you later," Darnell said as he walked away.

"What you do that for?" I asked as Kabrian approached.

"Aint no dudes being around you while I'm here."

I just laughed, and we joked around until the sermon was to start. I loved having my cousin around.

School had started, I was in middle school this year, 7th grade. I decided this year I wanted no drama. I began hanging out with Dajia a lot. We had so much fun over the summer, why not continue that into the school year. I didn't have any classes with Dajia, but I did with Zelle. This gave us a chance to make up. I saw Darnell through the hallway sometimes busy he was busy with his new friends. We still hung out before and after church. At lunch, I sat down to eat with Zelle and Tiana. I saw Dajia and waved her over.

"Zelle, Tiana, this is Dajia. We met over the summer, our God-parents are roommates", I said.

"Hey, I am Dajia."

"We know that she just told us your name," Tiana said.

"Tiana---," I started.

"Well I wanted to introduce myself anyway," Dajia said.

"Girl don't nobody care…" Zelle placed her hand over Tiana's mouth.

"Ke I am going to go sit with Samantha, so I don't have to slap this bitch."

Tiana stood up to scrap, but we convinced her to let it go. As we were walking to our next class. Tiana and Dajia saw each other in passing.

"Stupid Bitch," Dajia mumbled.

Tiana snapped. All I saw was arms swinging. Next thing I saw was Tiana had Dajia slammed up again the band hall wall. Mr. Wright broke up the fight. They both were sent to the office. Tiana looked fine, but Dajia had a black eye. I felt so bad, I was the one that introduced them.

My next and last class was athletics. Everyone had to complete a fitness test in 6th grade to take it into athletics. I wanted to play basketball to be closer to my dad. He played in high school. I heard he was good. Somehow, I made it. I shared this class with a few girls I knew Zaria, Jessica, Brianna, and Niya. After bonding, during a ten-minute run around the gym and our mutual hate for Coach Phillips, I was able to make up with Zaria and Niya. We all just had misunderstandings.

The year progressed with little to no drama. I bonded more with the athletics girls during basketball season. This was my first year playing, we pretty good. Until Valentine's day, I was waiting on Zelle and Tiana so we could go through the snack bar line. They had stuffed crust pizza and wings today. They were taking longer than usual to arrive today, so I got in line by myself. I was standing there minding my own business.

"Hey, is your name Kennadi?"

"Yeah?!?", I replied. I was confused, I had no idea who this guy was.

"I heard your mom just be killing niggas," he said.

I stood there puzzled.

He continued, "I heard a nigga came at her and (POW)." He made the sound effect as he raised his pretend gun and shot into the air.

I said nothing, I turned and left I ran to the nearest bathroom and just cried. I skipped the rest of lunch. I ran into Zelle and Tiana on the way to athletics. My eyes red, with a somber expression. They asked what was wrong I didn't want to talk about it. I hadn't told them about my mother and father, and I didn't plan to. They told me why they were late. Turns out they were hanging out with their boyfriends. Great! I went through the motions today in athletics, I just wanted to go home. After school I saw the guy again, he was laughing and joking with his friends.

I guess seeing him increased my rage. I walked over and hit him as hard as I could. I broke his nose. There was blood everywhere. I stared at him as he held his nose. His friends stood there in awe. Next, think I know I am being hauled to the office by the principal. My mother was called to come to get me, and I was told I would have to go to in-school suspension (ISS) for a few days. On the way home, my mom fussed and complained about having to take off work to come to get me. I lied about why I punched that boy. I did not want my mom to feel bad. It had been twelve years, but people still would not let it go. When we got home, I saw gifts on my bed. My mom had bought me A heart cake, card, bear, and balloons. I was grateful but just slid them away. Valentine's day was ruined for me.

I sat out my ISS time. It was so boring, my only entertainment would be when Zelle and Tiana would call my name from the halls, and the teacher chased them away. If I learned one thing that was, I did not want to end up back in there. For the rest of the year, I started keeping my head down. In English, we were learning about slavery and important people in black history. I had to do research over Sojourner Truth. I loved her speeches and poetry, she had inspired me to write my own poetry. After the fight poetry helped me a lot, it allowed me to express myself. People began to talk about me, I was accused of being manly. My best friends tried to shield me from the rumors, but they couldn't protect me from everything. On our way to class, there was a group of guys walking behind us.

"Man, Jessica looking good today," said Oliver.

"Right, Monique too. Those micro braids make every girl look better", said Brian.

(Group Laughs)

"Man look at Kennadi. That bitch built like a linebacker", said Braylon.

(Laughs)

I looked back to show I heard him. Dekorian was the only one not laughing. His grandmother and my aunt were friends. We knew each other outside of school. Tiana looked at me with a sympathetic face. I said nothing. I tried to block it out like I heard nothing. I already knew I wasn't beautiful. I was taller than all the guys, I had crooked teeth (thanks to my thumb sucking habit), I was born with this large mole, and my hair was now a brittle mess. My mom said I was growing up and should have my hair done. She took me to a beautician. This lady permed my hair with a super perm. My hair still hasn't grown back properly. I just could not believe he said it in front of everybody. We used to be friends, or so I thought. I forced myself to keep it together for the rest of the day, but when I got home, I would write and cry. I should have punched him in the mouth. I just didn't want to get in trouble again. This would be the start of my crushed self-esteem. I started to hate myself. I began to eat away my feelings. That cake I mentioned earlier was devoured entirely. Food wouldn't talk about me or put me down, it only made me feel better.

The Party

Niya was having an end of the year school party, everyone was invited. I wasn't sure about going. I had already dealt with crappy situations this year, why add to it? Tiana and Zelle talked me into it. Tiana would come over my house, and we would get dressed together, then head to the party.

"Hey girl, come on in," I said as I showed her to my room.

"Dang, what happened in here?"

"I don't know what to wear. You look cute". I said

"Girl you better throw on some jeans and a cute shirt like I did. Where your mom?"

"She is in the back getting ready. I think she is going out tonight."

My mom and brother were getting dressed, it was the weekend, and we all had someplace to be. Most of the time we would get dressed together while dancing and singing. Our theme song was Mr. Hit Dat. I took Tiana's advice and wore some jeans and a top.

"Y'all ready?", my mom asked.

"Yes," I replied.

We arrived at the party. It was at their apartment's clubhouse. The music was so loud, you could hear it in the car with windows up. We went through the clubhouse doors; the party was packed. There were pink balloons everywhere, the lights were dim, and everyone was hyped. We spotted Zelle in a corner. She had her cousin with her, Breontay.

"Hey y'all, what's up?" I said.

"Nothing, this party crazy," Zelle said

"Hey Breontay," I said.

No Response

"Let's go dance", Zelle said.

"I will later," I said. I loved to dance. In fact, I used to stay up at night and dance in the dark to music, it was peaceful.

"Okay."

Zelle and Breontay went dancing. Tiana and I went to go get some punch. Tiana could dance too, it was just different dancing in front of people. We just grabbed a plate and watched everyone dance. Tiana was cracking on people until it was time for a dance contest.

"Alright Y'all, let's see who gone get it the best? Winners gets $50", said Ms. Adrienne.

It was Niya party, so she chooses to battle Tiana. Tiana and I just looked at each other, she got up and walked to the middle of the floor. I followed her to watch. I knew she didn't want to but being called out was embarrassing. It started by Tiana doing a move, she busted out the chicken head. Niya retaliated with some pop lock move. The crowd cheered, Tiana began to dance harder to come back, but Niya on when she did some fancy move and flaunted her birthday money in Tiana's face. Tiana was upset, she left to get some air, Breontay followed her. Next up was Niya versus Tawnya. Tawnya did a vibrating move, and Niya lost. I went to check on Tiana. When we returned, Tawnya had won the contest. The party was back to its regular function. Everyone was again doing what they wanted. I looked at the dance floor and spotted Darnell dancing with my cousin Ty'Quesha. I rolled my eyes. Niya spotted me.

"Ke, I haven't seen you dance all night," said Niya

"Yeah, I just haven't felt like it."

"Well now is the time come on," she said. She pulled me to the dance floor, I just stood there. "If you don't dance, I am not inviting to you to any more parties."

I manage to do a burst of dance moves, not sure what I did because my adrenaline was rushing. I didn't know what my body was doing. After I was done, I ran off the floor. I went to look for Tiana and Zelle since the party was coming to an end. Tiana had left with Zelle and Breontay. I stood outside for a little while. Braylon and his friends came out.

"Kennadi, what you doing out here?", Oliver said

"Nothing waiting on my ride."

"I saw you dancing," he replied.

"I don't care if she can dance or not, she still manly," Braylon said.

Humiliated, I walked back into the party. I hated Braylon. I was so sick of Braylon and his comments, I don't know why he despised me so much. Why was he such an asshole? The party cleared as people left. Turns out the ride I was waiting on would not show.

"Ke, I will take you home," said Mrs. Adrienne

"Okay, thanks."

"Can I spend the night," Niya asked

"Yeah ma shouldn't care. She not there anyway."

Her mom dropped us off. We got dressed for bed, I gave her a shirt to wear.

"I'm still mad. How could I lose?"

"You gotta admit Tawnya killed that move."

"Whatever," she said.

74

I tried to be there for Niya. However, Braylon's comments were on my mind. Maybe I was manly. We laid down to go to bed after talking more about the party. She started that thing she did with rubbing up against me. Tonight, I was for it; I wanted more. Why not, everyone thought I was manly anyway, maybe it was time I embraced it. She kissed me. This time I rolled her on top of me and held her waist. I put my tongue down her throat and pulled her close. She went down to suck on my nipples. Then she made her way to my womanly parts. She licked, sucked, and nibbled on my essence, the feeling swallowed my body whole. I began to shake, I had to stop her. I pushed her off and returned the favor and then some. I spelled her full name with my tongue while sucking in-between the letters. Her legs began to shake as they wrapped around my head. She pulled me up. I kissed her as I placed my fingers inside her until she shivered again, and I felt her fluids run down my hand. I laid beside her, and she put her arm across me before we fell asleep.

The next morning my mom woke us for breakfast and told us her mom would be coming to get her soon. We got up, ate, took a shower, and watched TV in my room while waiting on her mother.

"Ke, I had fun last night," Niya said.

I smiled, "me too."

(Honk) her mom was outside.

She grabbed her stuff and kissed me on the way out. I didn't know exactly how I felt about everything, but I was happy. We had agreed not to tell anyone, we both were involved in the church, and we knew what happened to people like us. Maybe it was just a phase, things may change. At least the summer break was starting so we

75

wouldn't see each other for a while, which gave me time to process what just happened.

Aiden

That summer I spent mostly laying around and playing video games with my brother. My god- mom had spoken with my mother and she would be coming to get me again. I packed my bags. I opened the garage, Tina had rented a minivan. As I approached the car, I saw two new faces. Deaunna and Aiden; they were Alicia's siblings. Deaunna was tall and curly, with long wavy hair, she was mixed like Alicia. Aiden was something different. He was white with dreads and a body made from perfection. He helped me put my bags in the car, he muscles everywhere. I spoke to everyone and got in and sat by Dajia. Aiden smiled he had a gold grill. He was something sexy. When we arrived at the house, they told us that the next day we would be going to see Christopher Brown in concert. We all screamed, at least all the girls. I immediately ran to go get my outfit together. I was trying to appear more girly, so I pulled out a blue-jeaned skirt, blue camouflaged came that matched be blue camouflaged bathing gapes, and a white V-neck top. My mom had bought me some green contacts that I was dying to wear, I was wearing those.

"Ughhhh!", Dajia yelled.

"What's wrong Dajia?"

"I ain't got nothing to wear," she said.

I looked through her bag and pulled out a white collared shirt with a rhinestone playgirl bunny, blue jean gauchos, and white wedged sandals.

That night Alicia and Tina would go out for one of their friend's birthday. Deaunna and Aiden were to watch us. That nice we ate pizza danced and played video games. As everyone was taking turns showering and getting ready for bed. Aiden asked me to come outside.

"You got a boyfriend?", Aiden asked.

"No, I don't really do well in that area."

"What? I don't see why not When I saw you come out of that garage, I was like damn she fine", he responded.

"You don't look so bad yourself," I said.

I sucked at flirting, but Aiden had me blushing. I was shocked that a guy was into me. Especially one this fine. I was always teased about my features it felt good to be wanted. My phone beeped it was Darnell. He told me he was going to be moving to Dallas this summer. I felt like this was my last chance. I walked back inside and texted him.

"Hey Darnell"

"What you doing?", he asked.

"Nothing, I need to ask you something…"

"What's up?"

"Will you be my first?", I asked.

"For real?"

"Yeah"

No reply, or at least I don't remember getting one. I fell asleep waiting.

The next day was the concert. It was all of that, our god-parents had bought us front row tickets. We danced to Huuey, sand with Moniqua, and finally Christopher Brown's time to perform and put on a show. We laughed, danced, and fought over who we thought he was looking at; we really enjoyed ourselves.

Later that night, Aiden told me to check Mindspace. He had written me a message.

Watching you dance tonight had me feeling some way.

Really, how? What did you want to do to me? I replied.

This is how we would communicate without given off hints to my god mom and his sister about our relationship. The next day we went to the pool. Alicia and Tina stayed behind to barbeque. Aiden and I were openly flirting. I would get on his back to play chicken. By the looks, we were getting I am sure everyone noticed. When it was time to go, we lingered behind everyone else. He picked me up and sat me on a ledge. His body between my legs. He pulled me in and planted his lips on mine. I felt the rise in his pants. I said we should go before they notice we were not there. I pushed him away and ran to catch up with the others. After we were all cleaned up and ready for dinner. Tina and Alicia informed us we would be going to North Carolina for her nephew's birthday party. He had it at a teen club, and Soulja would be performing. I had never left the state before, and I was ready to go.

Busted

Getting to North Carolina would be a long trip. We took pictures by every state sign we passed. When we finally arrived, we approached this large ranch house (describe house). After we got settled Alicia's sister took us to the underground mall, after dinner, we went back to the house. I crashed, I was tired. The next morning, we would play around until it was time to go to the teen club.

While everyone was getting ready, Aiden and I were talking in the kitchen. His back was to the door he walked up to kiss me. I saw Alicia's sister, and I stepped back. She looked at us suspiciously and walked out. A little while later we backed into the car and headed out. Before we left Aiden and I had snuck into the liquor cabinet, at the party, I was feeling good. We walked in, everybody was eyeing us. Most likely because we were not from there and we were not dressed like everyone there. I don't care as soon as my song came on, I started dancing like I would in my room alone at night. This tall, dark guy with long twisted locks approached me. I was not used to anybody being taller than me. He was looking good from head to toe. I completely forgot about Aiden now and, I started dancing with him. After a while Dajia grabbed me.

"Girl go talk to Aiden," she said.

"What why?"

She pointed, "That's why."

I looked over, he was sitting against the wall. He was clearly upset. I walked over to him.

"Aiden"

"Man, I ain't got nothing to say. How you gone play me?", he said.

"I was just dancing, it's nothing."

"Whatever," he said.

I whispered, "I can make it up to you."

I then gave him a lap dance in that chair he happened to be sitting in. I stayed with him for the rest of the night. Alicia called to let us know she was outside. The group had split up. I went to find Dajia. She was in the back kissing some dude. I told her we had to go. We all ran outside waiting on the van. Before I knew it, I fight broke out. There was weave everywhere. I didn't know what happened, but I would be happy we would be leaving soon. The cops arrived as we pulled off.

The next morning Alicia told us we would be leaving. We said our goodbyes and piled our things into the van. On the way back, Peter got sick and threw up all over my shirt. Tiff pulled over to clean up and so I could change. I grabbed a shirt out the back I took my shirt off and switched into another one. Aiden smiled, I inched closer to him. Then I noticed Alicia eyeballing us, so I hurried to put the shirt on and got in the car. I slept on and off the rest of the trip. I wondered if Alicia saw anything, was she reading our body language? We finally made it home, and due to how late it was we crashed.

I woke up to commotion going on in the back room. Looks like I was the last one up. I looked over all the kids were sitting on the couch, except Aiden.

I went to go pee, the commotion stopped. As soon as I opened the door.

"Ke come here," Tina screamed.

"Yes?"

"What is going with you and Aiden and don't you say nothing, Alicia's sister already told us what she saw," Tina said

Oh, crap I was thinking. I looked at Aiden, he gave me that eye, so I lied. "Nothing is going on with us," I said

They kicked us out and asked everyone in one by one. I guess somebody said something because it all had come out.

"So, I am going to ask again?" My god mom meant business this time. I had never seen her so mad. No not angry, disappointed.

"Okay," I said. I told them everything.

 I left them with the Mindspace messages they read them as I packed my bags and preparing for my god mom to take me home. On the ride home, I didn't say anything. She met my mom halfway. She didn't even say bye to me.

On the trip home my mom explained to me why everyone was distraught. Turns out Aiden was in trouble with the law in his hometown. He had apparently seduced a "minor" there and was facing charges. You see Aiden was 21; I was thirteen. Alicia was trying to convince people he was innocent until me. I couldn't believe it. He didn't seem like a predator to me. Maybe I was just distracted at the fact that a guy showed me some attention. My mom then informed me I couldn't go visit my god mom unless Aiden wasn't there. I didn't go back that summer. However, Neisha and Dajia would call to check on me. Neisha informed me that

Alicia was still upset with me, so they made sure she was gone before they reached out.

Since I wouldn't be going to Irving anytime soon, I decided to spend the rest of the summer entertaining myself at the Guys and Girls Club. It was a recreational center where most of the kids would hang out over the summer. School was out, but my mom still had to work. If I wasn't at my granny's, I was there. If I want watching basketball games or playing in the game room, I snuck into the adult lounge to watch music videos. I was so tall they never asked how old I was. In the game, the lounge is where I started hanging with Brittney. Brittney was in my athletics class, while she did not play basketball, she ran track. We all shared the same locker room. Brittney was shorter than me and had a banging body, she was also funny. All the guys at school liked her. One day after being the Guys and Girls Club she invited me to come with her to her friend's house; I went. At first, we were sitting in the living room watching music videos when the doorbell rang. Four guys walked in. Giovanni, Derek, Martin, and Alex. I noticed everyone paring off. I was left sitting on the couch with Dianna. After the Aiden situation, I was not looking for any dude. After he realized this was not going anywhere, he left and so did I. I walked over to my aunt's house. Turns out she lived in the same apartments.

After my mom got off, she came to take me home. It was the weekend so she would be going out tonight. I spent that night at home writing in my diary and creating poetry until I dozed. That Sunday I saw my cousin Kabrian at church, only today he didn't really speak to me. I guess he really didn't have to lurk since Darnell had moved to a different city.

"Hey---"

"Hey Ke, I'm gonna talk to you a little later," he said

"Ooookay!"

He turned around and continued flirting with the twins. This would happen several times. It became the usual that every time I saw him, he was entertaining some girl. The next time I would see him would be at the scrimmage football game right before school started back.

"Ke," he said approaching me with open arms.

I said nothing and walked right past him.

"What's her problem." He asked my mom.

"You know she crazy, how you doing?", my mom replied.

The conversation continued, but I was no longer in hearing distance.

I went to go find my friends, we hung out into the game was over. I didn't tell them about what happened at my god-mom's. We just watched the game.

Freshman

School was back in session, it was a relief after the summer I had I was looking forward to it. However, I was nervous. This would be my first year of high school and this year we had to start wearing uniforms. This year my mom dropped me off at school instead of me riding the bus. When I arrived at school, I met up with Layla. Layla was a girl I had met last year in athletics. She had the clearing chocolate skin I had ever seen. She was boogie, but ratchet. She wore all the name brands but was quick to put you in your place if you tried to come for her. Layla was at the top of the stairs. As soon as we reached the top, a fight broke out beneath us. From above it looked like it was the Mexicans versus black people, but it really was a gang fight. Five different fights were going on at once. After principals broke it up, everyone was expected to go straight to class. High school was intimidating. I was used to going to school with those one grade above me, but not two or three grades above me. I had a few classes with Zelle and Tiana. My biggest surprise was I had a class with Niya. We didn't speak or hang out much at school, but every weekend she was at my house. The rest of the day was cool, a lot of walking. I do not know how they expected me to get from one class to another in three minutes. Presetting my locker combination helped, but I still had to rush to be in class on time. Last period was athletics, I loved this. This way I wouldn't have to walk around the whole day smelling like sweat. It was the off-season for basketball, so we ran drills to help us perfect our skills

After school, I got home I crashed on the bed. I may have been older, but I still wanted my nap. My mom was home. Her new boyfriend was over, so I knew not to expect to see her until after he left. My brother was at my granny's, his school was closer to her house. She would bring him home later. I was watching Sister Brother when the phone rang. It was Darnell, I hadn't heard from him since the move.

"Kennadi, what you doing?"

"Nothing, you? It's been a while. How is everything?", I asked.

He spent most of the call telling me about his new home, school, and what he had been up to over the summer. I listened, I loved hearing his voice. We didn't mention the text conversation, and I was happy we didn't. My mom finally came out of the room. I guess Jodi had gone out the back door. I didn't like him, I felt like he was using my mom, but she was too blind to see it.

"Kennadi, how was your first day of high school?", mom asked.

"It was okay, a lot going on, but I will get used to it."

"Yeah, adjusting takes time.", she said. "Marq how was your day?"

My brother had finally been released from BAEP and could continue regular school again.

"It's aight ma," he said.

They continued talking about his adjustment back into regular classes. After dinner, I went to figure out which combination of school uniforms I was going to wear tomorrow.

I went to the auditorium today, after the fight we were the staff was stricter about us being in the auditorium or cafeteria. I choose the auditorium; fewer people were in there. I saw Justine and sat down to talk to her. Next thing I know a group of upperclassmen girls walked in and sat behind us. I knew one of the girls from church Reese Talon.

"Kennadi, were you trying to get with Giovanni?"

"No, why," I responded.

"That's not what he said. I'm Karmen, his girl."

"Okay---," I said.

She called Giovanni on the phone. "She said you are lying," she then gave me on the phone.

"I did not try to get with you," I said.

"I know she my girl just go along with it," he said

If Karmen had been smart, she would have put this call on speakerphone. I started to reply when Karmen snatched the phone. She continued speaking as she walked away. Her minions bumped me with their shoulders as they walked past me. I was just happy they were leaving. I was big and when confronted would stand my ground, but, I did not like confrontation. It made me nervous, and my hands would shake. I was not very social and could never find the right words to say. I tried to forget about that morning and went on with my day. That day people kept running up to me telling me how Karmen charged me up or asking me about rumors relating to Giovanni. I did my best to laugh it off or change the subject. Nothing happened, I don't know why people were so interested in this situation.

A few weeks passed, and that situation was put to rest. In my math class with Niya, there was Amber. I had not really seen much of her since elementary school, last time I remember interacting with her was that fight in fourth grade. After sharing the same class, we became friends. She had invited me to come over this weekend, I was down, I mean why not why not. Zelle had become popular and was hanging with a different crowd. Tiana had moved to California to stay with her sister for a little while. The week would pass, and it would be time to go to Amber's. I arrived at Amber's house. She lived around the corner from Niya. She showed me around the house. Her mom was nice. That day we mostly went through her closet mixing and matching party outfits and played in some make-up. She had a frog game. I had never heard of it before. We played that up until dinner. After dinner, we went to her room to watch a movie. She put the film on then came down and sat next to me. After a few minutes, she grabbed my arm and put it around her. I hesitated and looked at her. She looked back at me and smiled. She was hot. So, I left it there, she then put her arm around my waist. I don't know if I looked like a boy or what, I was always drawing some girl's attention. I enjoyed it though, my mom was always busy and with my dad out of the picture it felt good. Plus, guys didn't seem into me. Midway through the movie she looked at me and kissed my cheek. I knew where this could go. I pulled back.

"What's wrong?", Amber asked.

"Um---Nothing," I said. I couldn't let her know I was thinking about Niya.

"I like you she said don't you like me?", she asked

"I think you are cute."

"Well, what's wrong?", she asked again.

I guess I don't belong to Niya. Plus, who would tell her? I won't. I pulled her in and kissed her. She rolled on top and straddled me. We kissed zealously. I pushed her backward and unbuttoned her pants. I slid my hand down her panties. She grabbed my hand and pulled it deeper inside her. I was on my way down to taste her ice cream. (Boom) Her older cousin busted in the door. Luckily, the room was still dark.

I rolled off her quick. Her cousin hit the lights, and Amber rolled over to play sleep. I pretended as if I was watching the movie.

"What yall doing?", Monica asked.

Amber didn't answer.

"I'm watching It, it's about to go off now though," I said

"This girl always falling asleep on her company," she said

"My brother does the same thing I joked truth is I was nervous I hope she couldn't tell I was lying. It's okay. I am going to sleep after this go off", I said

"Alright," she said as she shut the door.

Amber rolled over. "Sorry about that."

"It's all good," I said rolling over to sleep. I didn't know what she was thinking, but that was a close one. I was going there again the next morning I called my mom to come to get me early.

Niya kept calling me all weekend. I never answered. I felt so guilty, but why? We were not a couple. Sunday at church I didn't know what to think. I tried to talk to Kabrian, but he was preoccupied with the twins. He had been doing that a lot lately. He started blowing me off for these girls. I confronted him

"Why do you keep blowing me off?"

"I am not---"

"Yes, you are! Every time I try to talk to you, you always say later Ke. You ever think I really needed to talk to you? Maybe it's important", I said.

"I—"

"Whatever!", I yelled.

I walked away. I had no interest in someone who did not have time for me, I was so sick of feeling abandoned by people. From then on out I wouldn't speak to him when I saw him. He always asked my mom what was up with me or why I was always tripping. I don't know if she told him, but I didn't stick around to hear.

At school the next week something was off. Niya wouldn't talk to me, and Amber would avoid me. Soon I would learn. That weekend Niya came over as usual. She rang the doorbell my mom let her in. She came into my room. I approached to kiss her, and she pushed me away.

"What's wrong, why you mad at me?"

"You think I'm stupid," she said.

"What?!?"

"I know about Amber," she said.

"She told you?"

"No, I can tell by the way she been acting," she responded.

I put my foot in my mouth, if I knew she had no proof, I would not have said anything. "Nothing happened."

"Whatever," she said.

"Naw really," I pulled her close. Her arms were folded. "She kissed me, and I pushed her away."

"That bitch...", she started.

I kissed her to shut her up.

"That ain't gone work," she said.

I hit my remote and put on the music stereo. Next, I pushed her against the door and pulled down her jeans. Even if she wanted to fight me, I knew she wouldn't, I knew her weakness. I lifted one leg and put it over my shoulder as I sucked on her clit until her other leg got weak. I then put that leg on my shoulder and lifted her up. Licking her essence while carrying her to the bed. Her hands were pulling my hair. She started throwing it back at my tongue, she was close. I laid her down and grabbed her breast while I was tongue deep. She let go and came. I rolled over held her close.

"I'm sorry about Amber."

She was silent she rolled over and kissed me. "I love you."

I didn't say anything. How could I? I didn't love her. I had only loved one person. Darnell. I just put my arm around her and let her sleep. Niya and I were back on good terms.

First Heartbreak

Basketball season had started, and I was doing my thing. Zaria was the star player, but after she moved up to varsity, I was able to shine. The first game I scored 25 points. I was in the zone. Through all the noise I could hear my mom and grandfather cheering me on. This was a big deal; my grandfather had not been feeling well. In the locker room, the team was excited, we high fived and danced as we changed. This excitement wouldn't last long. We arrived at the house after the game to find out our home was broken into. Our neighbor was a cop. He saw the people who robbed us, but thought nothing of it, because he had seen him before, Jodi. He took our brand-new plasma and my mom's gold necklace. My mom filed a report, but I knew she was heartbroken. That night I fried up some chicken tenders and fried okra for dinner. It was my brothers favorite, my mom had not left the room since she filed the police report, but I made her a plate just in case.

"Great game last night, but I have some bad news," she said

"What's up coach?"

"Many teams in the district do not have enough players for three teams so there will be no freshman team. Just varsity and junior varsity", she said.

My stomach sunk. I did not want to play with the upperclassmen. They were way more advanced. Most of the team was upset about this decision, many felt like they would not get to play anymore. That weekend I laid up in Niya lap and vented about it as she played with my hair. She wasn't really listened she seemed preoccupied on her phone. She told me she couldn't stay over tonight. She left after dinner. I thought it was strange but whatever.

(Ring)

"I about to send you something," Darnell said.

"What is it?"

"Just hang up I will call you right back," he said.

A few minutes passed, and my cell beeped. I opened the file. "I love her like money, pussy, weed…". It was a song by Lil Twayne.

(Ring)

"Did you hear it?", he asked.

"Yeah never heard it before."

"I mean the lyrics. Did you listen to the lyrics?", he asked.

"Yeah."

"That's how I feel about you," he said.

I blushed I guess underneath all his thuggish ways he was sensitive. "I love you too," I said.

Monday at school I found out where Niya was. As I mentioned before small town means everyone knows everybody's business. As I was walking to the first period, I stopped by my locker to get my materials.

"Kennadi." It was Amber.

"What?"

"Guess you need to get your girl," she said.

"Who?"

"Niya"

"Why?", I asked.

"Everybody talking about her. She got caught sneaking Ryan into her room. Her mom went off and beat Niya all upside the head", she said.

"Dang that's messed up. They should know Mrs. Adrienne doesn't play", I said. Hiding my real emotions of betrayal. I wonder if this how she felt after the entire Amber situation?

"Well, I gotta get to class. I will see you at lunch", she said as she walked away.

I slammed my locker and went to class. Niya couldn't even look at me. It didn't matter I had nothing to say to her anyway. Basketball season was ending, we had our last game on Friday. Everyone was more concerned with favorites. Favorites was Valentine's day school dance, I was excited and nervous about it. For one it was on a day that I hated and two I had to wear a stupid dress. After school Niya called.

"What?"

"I'm sorry," she said.

"Man, I ain't tryna hear dat," I replied.

"I really liked Ryan, and I had never been with a guy before…"

She continued talking, but I had zoned out. Never been with a guy before? Were there other girls in the picture? I ain't got time. Look, Man, dis ain't working. It's over. Click. Back then we had flip phones hanging up was so it and felt so good. The sound of the telephone slamming together made the moment even more gratifying.

(Boom)

I heard a commotion outside my door. I opened it and saw my mom being dragged by her boyfriend. As soon as she spotted me, she alerted me that they were playing, and it was okay. I shut my door and laid down to call Layla. If this was Niya idea of love, I wondered what was Darnell's?

"Hey!"

"What's up?", she asked.

"I need you to do me a favor, Call Darnell and flirt with him on three-way."

"Darnell from middle school, yall still talk?"

"Yeah, just see what he say," I said

"Alright, what's the number?"

I gave her the digits.

"Hold on she switched lines, and when she came back, I heard ringing."

"Hello"

"Darnell?"

"Yeah who dis?"

"Layla"

"Oh, what's up? How you get my number?", he asked.

"A friend…"

They talked about basic stuff for a while then. "What's up with you and Kennadi?"

"We just friends, what's up with you though?", he asked.

Layla paused but then proceeded to talk about her boyfriend. I hung up that's all I needed to hear. Both so-called people that loved me were full of shit. My best friend Zelle had moved on, and Tiana was in California I felt so alone. To make matters worse, I could now hear my mom's moans through the wall. I cut on the studio and blasted it until I fell asleep. When I woke my brother was home, but my mom was still cooped up in her room. I called him to the living room, and we played vice city. I then went to make us some dinner fried chicken strips and fries. Thank God for deep fryers, that's all I knew how to make. After dinner, we washed up and got ready for school. I ironed me and my brothers' clothes and laid down to watch the Fresh Prince of Los Angeles until I dozed.

The next morning, I met up with Layla to talk about favorites. I didn't mention Darnell, and neither did she. The situation was embarrassing enough. Then we talked about the game tonight. Since it was the last game, they liked to put on a whole production called Jam the Gym. Ham the gym is where all the basketball teams play on the main gym floor, during the games, music is played. At the last Jam the Gym Byron Bell dunked on the goal and broke it. Glass shattered everywhere. Everyone ran to the floor to get a piece.

A few weeks passed, Basketball season was over, and favorites was tonight. I wore a black dress with a split up the side. I had no date or anyone to go with, so I was going to take my brother.

(Ring)

"Hey bitch!"

"Tiana?!?"

"Who else, what you doing?"

"Getting ready for favorites, you?"

"My sister and I moved back to Texas, so I am coming," she said.

"Yesss, I was excited Okay I will meet you in front of the school at 7pm.", I said.

"Aight, I will tell Zelle too," she said, "Bye!"

Zelle and I had not been talking much, but our girl was back so we would get over it. I arrived at the school for the dance. Tiana and Zelle were waiting for me. I ran and squeezed Tiana, I missed her so much. We walked into the dance. There was a line for pictures, so we decided to skip them for now, plus we each had our own cameras. We got some food and took a seat. We laughed and talked for a while until our song came on by John, Sit Low. Everybody ran to the dance floor. As we were dancing, I felt someone grab my butt, I turned around, and it was Oliver, he smiled at me and kept walking. I just ignored him and continued dancing with my girls. We practically danced the night away. After favorites, I went home instead of the after party. I was tired, and my feet were killing me, but I had a good time.

(Ring)

"Open the garage," said my mom.

As I opened the garage, all I saw was my mom's car come flying around the corner. She managed to park the car and come crawling around to the garage door. "Ma?"

She was talking, but I didn't understand. I quickly shut the garage and ran to help her up. I put her arm around my neck, and we staggered to her room. She was drunk. I helped her out of her clothes and put her into the shower.

"Thank you," she slurred.

"Welcome," I said and left out. I guess she managed to clean herself and get in the bed. I went back to check on her, and she was knocked out. I am happy my brother was at my granny's, so he didn't witness this.

The next morning, I sat in the auditorium waiting for class to start. Approaching me was the usual group of girls, but today there were more.

"There she go," Ke said.

(snickers)

"Man, some people looking rough today, they cheap weave didn't last a minute after that dance," Karmen said.

I knew they were talking about me. My mom did my hair for the dance. She tried her best, but she was not a pro, and we couldn't afford to have it done professionally at the time. My tracks were slipping, and my real hair had started to peak through. I had done my best to fix it for school, but I guess I had failed.

(Laughs)

Justine gave me a sympathetic look. I just sat there I didn't engage.

"Oliver told me somebody didn't have on draws at the dance either," Joy said.

This confirmed they were talking about me. My mom made me where a thong to the dance. She didn't want my panty line to show through my dress. I still did not engage. I just wanted to cry. I don't know why this girl had it out for me. I already explained I wasn't interested in her man. The bell rang, and I hurried off to class. I went through the motions for the rest of that semester in school. However, there was one guy who was into me, Ray. I should have been into him, he was the only guy taller than me in our class, but I wasn't. He would follow me to class. One day he even ran up and kissed me. Turns out this dude had a girlfriend.

"Kennadi," Layla said.

"Yeah."

"This is Ava," she said as she pointed to this girl.

I was confused. "Hi---"

"Say what you need to say," Layla said to Ava.

Apparently, this was Ray's girlfriend, and she had a problem with me. I didn't understand, shouldn't she be discussing these issues with him? He was the one following me around the school and leaving notes in my locker. He even cornered me trying to kiss me. I kicked him in the balls and ran away. I was not interested. I stood there to hear what she had to say but she said nothing, so I just walked away. I don't know why Layla tried to set up this ambush. I thought we were friends.

Kabrian

Over the summer I ran into my cousin Kabrian as I was walking with my aunt to her boyfriend's house

"What's up girl?", he said as he came to give me a hug and kissed my forehead."

I didn't resist I missed him so much, and it was hard to be made when you felt so down. "How you doing?", I said

"I'm good---"

He barely got the words out before we heard screaming. I ran into the house to see what was going on. My aunt had caught her sons' father with his side chick.

"Bitch try me," aunt Tiff said.

"He doesn't want you," the woman yelled.

My aunt's boyfriend said nothing he was quiet. My guess he was hoping my aunt didn't stab him with the knife she was holding.

(Clap)

My aunt went upside his head. I tried to grab her, so we could leave, but she was too strong. Kabrian came in, and we were able to get her out of the house. He calmed my aunt and had us leave before the cops arrived. As we walked back to my granny's, she was livid. I understood how she felt. She went inside and told my granny what was going on. I sat outside waiting for my mom to arrive.

"Ke I got good news, Tina coming to get you for fourth of July," she said.

"Really?!?"

I was excited and nervous at the same time. I hadn't been there since the incident and Dajia was mad at me because she caught me laughing at her hairstyle a few weeks ago. I was still willing to go. I loved visiting my god mom.

Weeks passed, and it was finally time to go. This time my mom dropped me off because she was going to meet up with her new boyfriend in Dallas. I hugged my mom goodbye and walked up to the apartment. Everyone was sitting around watching tv, it was awkward. However, I walked up to Dajia and apologized, I also complimented her outfit. We were back to talking as usual. That night out godparents decided we were old enough for the talk. They spoke to us about sex and mostly showed us pictures of diseases. They expressed the need for condoms, birth control, and STD's. They gave me way more information than the school health class. All they discussed was abstinence. After the presentation, the kiddos went back to the living room to eat pizza and watch movies.

"Ke," Tina said.

I walked back to the bedroom where they were.

"Sit down," she said.

The mood seemed serious, I was scared they were going to bring up the Aiden situation again. "Yes?!?"

They gave me the phone. "Hello?!?" It was my mom.

"Ke"

"What's wrong ma?" I could tell she was crying.

(sobbing)

"What, what's wrong?" I began to panic.

"Kabrian passed," she said.

My heart fell into my stomach. I jumped off the bed. "What happened? How?", I asked.

I didn't let her finish. I threw the phone and burst into tears. I couldn't believe it, my heart just ached. I ran outside to get some fresh air. A few minutes later Dajia came out to check on me. I laid over and cried in her shoulder. I didn't want to eat, I wanted to sleep, and never wake up. I got myself together and went to the bathroom. My eyes stung my face was red. I took some pills from my god moms medicine cabinet and went to sleep. That night around 3:00am I woke up crying Dajia sat beside me held me in her arms and rocked me I fell back asleep. When I woke up, I was still in her arms. I asked my God mom to take me home. The entire way home I just looked out the window and cried. I couldn't believe this I just couldn't. Not again, I was so sick of death.

When we arrived home, I ran into the house and hugged my brother. He was just as tore up as I was. That day we spent in my room listening to music and crying. A few days later we were to go to the wake. I hadn't seen a dead body in a long time. Not since uncle Steve. I walked in holding my brother to view the body. The sight of his hit me like a bag of bricks. My brother ran out into my grandmothers' arms. I froze staring at him, he was dressed in a purple suit. He looked as if he was sleeping, but his body was lifeless. There was a knot on his forehead. Maybe from the shooting or a fight before. I wasn't sure. I hated seeing him like that I ran out of the funeral home sobbing, I wasn't going to his funeral tomorrow; I couldn't do it. The rest of my family went, I stayed home. I cried for most of the day. I had to be delirious. At one point I looked up and thought I saw him smiling and waving to me as if he was saying goodbye. I grabbed the bottle of pain meds I took from my mom's cabinet and went to sleep.

I heard the funeral was beautiful. They were going to have a party in remembrance for him at the park next weekend. If I managed to pull myself together by then, so I would go. The morning of the party my mom took my brother and me to Brudon's to get shirts made. At the party, everyone had one Kabrian's face, and name was plastered everywhere. People gave speeches about fun times with him, then it was time to party. I don't remember much though. I had started drinking ever since I saw his body in the casket. Next, I would drink at Zelle's house when her mom wasn't home. My mom collected liquor bottles each time she went out, so I had easy access to alcohol. I would just fill the bottle up with water. My mom never noticed. The rest of that summer was a blur, I was at a lost, I didn't remember anything, I was just happy we made up beforehand. If we didn't that would be a pang of guilt I couldn't carry.

Building My Cocoon

This school year I decided I was going to be different. I had recently watched a documentary about the phases of butterflies. I admired how they went through stages of change and came out as something stronger and beautiful. I started dressing more like a girl. I was still drinking, however, in school, I had to be careful. I would empty water bottles and pour patron into the bottle. I would just sip on it through the day. It felt good, I didn't want to feel anymore. I just wanted to coast, I liked being numb. This year I was a sophomore, as I walked the halls, I saw familiar faces, one of them being Giovanni. I kept my distance though. Layla was in BAEP, so I had been hanging with Bella. She would do my hair and come over my house occasionally. She used my house as a cover as she snuck away with her boyfriend, Ethan. This time she asked me to go with her. Ethan had brought his friend. Ethan blew the horn, and we walked to the car, as we approached, I saw Giovanni. Ethan took Bella to get something to eat. They talked and kissed, Giovanni, and I just sat in the back.

"So how do you know Ethan?", I asked trying to relieve the awkwardness.

"We work together," he said.

"Doing what?", I asked.

"Something we can't discuss."

"Sell Drugs?", I asked.

He smiled and nodded

"My mom's boyfriend does as well," I said.

"Who I he?"

"Something we can't discuss," I replied.

He laughed, "You got jokes."

We arrived back at my house. Bella got out and ran around to kiss Ethan goodbye. I just got out and walked to the door.

Giovanni and I began bonding after this we would flirt and just talk about life. Giovanni was always getting in trouble with the law which made him even more attractive in my eyes. He eventually got kicked out of school and sent to BAEP. We still talked. What made me feel special is no matter where he was, he would always call. He even spoke to his grandmother about me. The problem was Karmen. I didn't know if they were still together or not. She always had something smart to say to me, and her minions were still harassing me.

(Ring)

"Kennadi it's for you," my mom screamed.

I wondered why someone would call my house instead of my cell. "Hello?"

"Kennadi?"

"Yeah, who is this?", I asked.

"Karmen."

Why is she calling me? Who gave her my number? My voice was shaky I was nervous. "What's up?"

"Look I ain't calling to start nothing," she said, "I just wanted to tell you that this mess over Giovanni has to end. So, we don't have any beef."

"Oh… Okay"

"So, we good?", she asked?

"Yeah."

"Aight, bye."

I hung up the phone my hands were shaking, but I smiled. It felt good to know I would no longer have to look over my shoulder at school. It was a relief. Plus, maybe now Giovanni and I could date…. Wrong. I was spending the night at my aunt's house when Giovanni called.

"Ke, I need to tell you something."

"What?"

He sounded nervous, "You gone be mad at me."

"What is it?"

"Well I was hanging out at Jodi's, and Kaydence came over," he said.

"Okay."

"Well… we ended up sleeping together", he said.

Silence. I wanted to hang up on him, but I admired his honesty. At least I didn't have to hear about it from somebody else. I didn't understand though, my own sister. I guess I couldn't be mad. No one really knew we had been talking the last few months. However, this fueled the hate for my sister even more. You see after Niya got caught fooling around with Ryan, I attempted to date a guy as payback. His name was Nick. He was a good guy, but let's be honest, he wasn't my type. Shortly after the break-up, I found out my sister had started dating him. I mean she asked if I still liked him the day before and if she could hook her "friend" up with him. I said she could. Zelle told me Kaydence was the "friend," but I didn't believe her, guess she was right. I really did not care about Nick, but it was the principal, and it was embarrassing. I remember walking to class with some classmates.

"Kaydence a hoe," said Kendra "I found out she was sleeping with my boyfriend."

"Man, yall better get off my sis--.", I started. I looked up and saw her kissing Nick.

"Whoa, now she with your man," said Brittney.

I didn't say anything after that what was I to say? She a yella- bone, had long curly hair. She was funny, hood, and mysterious. That's why no girls liked her, and I was no different. Boys were not the only reason I hated my sister, she was our father's baby. She got the chance to know our dad's side of the family with no judgment. When they saw her, they felt sympathy, she had lost her father. When they saw me, it was different. Not only was I a girl that lost her father. I was also the monster's daughter. I could never be innocent in their eyes. For all I know, they probably thought I was the blame for his death. If my mom wasn't worried about me, would she have tried to get the gun from my dad? Would he still be alive? Therefore, I halfway hated myself as well.

"Kennadi?"

I guess I got lost in thought. "Man bye!"

Even though he told me about my sister. I didn't care this dude had my nose wide open. So, when he called me later begging me to forgive him, I did. I know, I am stupid. That night Layla invited me to come to hang out. She picked me up, and we head out.

"Where we going?", I asked.

"To Giovanni house, he is having a get-together," she said.

Huh? I was wondering why he didn't mention it to me. "Oh okay," I said

We arrived there were a few other guys there. Layla had got us something to eat so she sat at the table. I sat on the couch. The music was on, and everyone was dancing and having a good time. Some lights flickered outside

"Ms. Trudy here! Run!", someone shouted.

Everyone ran towards the back of the house. I had never been here before, so I ran into a room in the back. The only way out was through a tall window. I jumped on a bed to get some bounce. I climbed through the window, ran across the backyard and jumped the gate. Layla had already arrived in the car she parked around back I ran to it, and we speed off to my house. I looked down at my leg, and my pants were ripped, I had cut my thigh. We arrived at my home. I hopped out the car to go get changed. When I came back out everyone that was at Giovanni house was now at my house, except for him. I figured he got caught by his mom. I let everyone in, and we all sat in the living room. I went into my room to change again, I had thrown on pajamas, but now that everyone was here, I wanted to put on clothes. Plus, it was like five dudes and me I was very uncomfortable. I looked for Layla, but I guess she was in the car still. As I was changing Giovanni walked in the room.

He hit the light I turned around, and I felt him grab me. He pushed me on the bed and started kissing me. He then pulled my pants down and forced himself inside me. It hurt like hell, I had never had sex before, at least with a guy. I was so uncomfortable, I just laid there. After a few minutes, he spoke.

"Man, if you don't make sounds or something I am leaving," he said.

How the hell was I supposed to know to make sounds? This did not feel good at all. Your first time was supposed to be unique, I didn't want him to leave because of me messing up. I imitated the sounds I had made when I was with Niya. Meanwhile, he grunted as he pushed inside me.

"Ahh, Oooo!"

"Pussy, Pussy," he grunted.

He rolled me over and attempted to go from the back. It hurt worse, so I rolled back over, he kept pounding me until he was done. Afterward, we got up, and he helped me make the bed. He then kissed me as we walked back to the living room. Everyone had left except for his friend Derek, who happened to be in the living room masturbating to my sounds. I walked them both out to the door, locked it, took a shower and went to bed.

The next morning, I woke up feeling sore. I recognized this soreness. The night I woke up after Marvin punched me in the head. I looked up information about your first time. All the articles mentioned bleeding. I wasn't bleeding, but I bleed that night. Marvin. Marvin had raped me. I ran to the restroom and threw up. All these years I thought I was a virgin, all these years. I cried, I felt so worthless. How could he take that moment from me? I reached for my bottle of alcohol under my bed and chugged the whole thing down. It wasn't working this time. I took out the knife I had under my bed and began to cut. I cut my thighs. I saw the blood, felt the warmness of it running down my legs, but that was it. I felt no pain. I cut three lines down each leg. It was peaceful. That weekend I alternated between cutting myself, drinking, and taking pills, but no matter what I did, I could not wrap my mind around what happened to me. Should I tell my mom? She had been through enough, and I didn't want to make things worse. It happened so long ago. Would anyone believe me? Could anything be done about it? I was also embarrassed. How did I not know I was raped until years later? I am so stupid, I began to cry again. My mom tried to call me for dinner, but I did not want to eat. I just stayed in my room and cried myself to sleep.

At school the next week I met up to talk to Layla, she had an attitude.

"What's wrong with you?"

"First your sister, then you. Both of yall full of shit!", she said.

"What?" I was legitimately confused. "What are you talking about?"

"Giovanni, both of y'all slept with my boyfriend," she said.

"Boyfriend? I have been talking to Giovanni for five months. He never mentioned you", I said.

"We have been together for three months, and he never mentioned you."

"Look I am sorry, I had no idea yall were together."

"Where do you think we were that night? Everyone was in the house because we were having sex in the car", she said.

"What?" I felt so disgusted. I had just had sex with someone, who just came out of someone else's pussy. On top of this, I just found out my first time wasn't my first time. I was raped, by my brother's dad. "I am sorry I didn't know yall were a couple. I am done with him", I said.

I would never talk to him again, I can't believe how stupid I was. I should have known if he were cheating on Karmen he would cheat on me. If he slept with my sister, he would sleep with anyone else. I will no longer look for love. Guys looked as girls as an opportunity, I would do the same.

Layla and I tried to put things Giovanni behind us, but that didn't last long. I had started talking to Shawn, she ended up sleeping with him. Okay, payback. I thought until it happened again with this guy named Logan. We became frenemies, and eventually, our friendship fizzled. I began to feel alone again, I had grown apart from all my friends. I felt like I was on autopilot more and more each day. I ran out of space to cut on my legs, so I began to cut my arms. Winter was coming I had quit basketball, and no one would see.

"You are cutting the wrong side," Zaria said as she pointed at my arm. "If you want to kill yourself you have to cut the other side."

Mesha looked at me as I pulled my sleeves down. I didn't respond. I just rolled my eyes and headed to the restroom. I was embarrassed, and I sunk into my depression. My own cousin did not even care about what I was feeling or why I was harming myself.

At home, my mom didn't notice anything. I had grown so far apart from my friends that I really didn't have anyone to really talk to. I was literally falling down a hole in life, and no one even noticed something was wrong. I became withdrawn and stayed to myself, my friends thought I was acting funny. They didn't realize I was so far gone out of my mind. The only person I really had during this time in my life was Rachel. She was my cousin. She would come down on the weekends to hang out with me. We would play video games and just enjoy each other's company. I never told her about Marvin. I didn't know how. I wanted to forget about it and with her, I could. Except when she was with her boyfriend.

I was running out of places to cut, so I found another outlet for my emptiness, sex. I slept with whoever was interested. At church, they preached about saving yourself and keeping your virtue until you married. My virtue had been stolen. Then I had slept with an asshole after that, it was a little late for me to hear that lesson. I continued to isolate myself from my family, friends, and my conscience. The only time I would feel was when someone was inside me. People would talk, but I didn't care. I slept with my friends' boyfriends and other girls' boyfriends as well. They needed to know no matter how much a person says they love you, they were lying. They didn't care about you at all, they were too self- absorbed. I never felt bad for any of the girls or caught feelings for any guys.

Micah was the guy I was screwing at the time. We knew what was up, we weren't a couple. When it started, we were strictly fucking buddies, no feelings needed. He lived right down the street from me. The only problem was he was my cousin's boyfriend. When Rachel would come down, I would go over there with them. I even sat in the room once as they had sex. Seeing him with her didn't bother me. I knew eventually we would get bored and I would move on to the next. Our friendship started to change. He started treating me differently, he didn't just hit and leave anymore. Whenever we had sex afterward, he would stay, and we would talk. Even after he went home, he would call, and we would stay on the phone all night. If I weren't at school, he'd stop by my house to make sure I was okay. I assumed he cared about me because I thought our encounters were secret. However, he told his friends about us.

Rachel came to visit. This time Micah's friend was at the house also. Rachel and Micah got into it, and I went to check on him. I chased him down the street to see what was going on. By the time I came back she was pissed and packing her bags as Angel was running out the door.

"What's wrong with you?"

"When were you going to tell me about you and Micah?", she asked.

Angel hating ass must have told Rachel what was going on I thought. "I wasn't. It didn't matter. It was before your anyways", I said.

"Well if I would have known about yall. I would not have gone there", she said.

"It's cool Rachel we were not into each other like that. Why are you packing?"

"This is a bit much, she said, "I called my mom, she is going to come to get me."

That was the last time my aunt came to visit me, she wouldn't answer my calls or speak to me. I became angry and lashed out at her because she was ignoring me.

Rachel?

Are you going to come back?

Bitch, I know you see my text.

Look Micah was nothing.

Rachel?

Man fuck you hoe, that's why I made that nigga cum without him even being inside me.

Stupid bitch.

At school Monday it seemed like everyone was whispering about me. I guess news had got out about that weekend. Micah avoided me. If I didn't feel anything before that hurt. I think he really liked my aunt. He wanted to be with her over me. I should have known better. One of the girls from athletics noticed us hanging out and asked him if he wanted to go out with me. He said no. I should have known then. He wanted me in private, but that was it. Another Giovanni, I guess the apple doesn't fall far from the tree. Micah and Giovanni were brothers. I had stopped sleeping with him after that. However, I kept drinking. One day I popped open my bottle in the auditorium. It made a loud pop, Justine and I jumped. It was so loud, or so I thought. I later found out that at the same time I was opening my bottle to fill my voids, another was taking his life to fill his. Someone had brought a gun to school and committed

114

suicide. I figured God was trying to get my attention or show me something. I took notice. In my mind I felt I was the only one dealing with issues in life, no one could understand, but I was wrong. This was my wake-up call. I stopped drinking and went back to a healthier way to express myself, poetry.

That summer, I asked my mom if I could go to my god mom for winter break just to get away. When I arrived, I was the only one where the rest of the crew had stayed with their families. This offered me a chance to focus on myself. I didn't have to drink here, there was nothing to avoid. I focused on my poems.

"What are you doing?", Alicia asked

"Writing poems."

"Mind if I look?", she said.

"She read over a few then handed them back."

She sat down and looked me in my eyes. "Are you okay?"

"Yeah---," I said. I was used to putting on a face for people and hiding my truths. It seemed like nobody really cared or choose to hide the negatives.

"Okay I was just checking," she said.

Tina and I went to dinner and when we returned there was an envelope on my bed. I open it, it was a letter from Alicia. It read:

Ke,

After reading over your poems, they seemed to be filled with dark emotions. You seem to value yourself based on how others see you. You are smart, kind, and more than enough. You do not need anyone's approval to know that you are great. Be your own light. Don't let the views of others mold you into a person that you do not know or do not like. It is okay to be yourself, to stand alone, and to not be in a crowd. Do not be a follower. I love you, and if you ever need to talk, I am here.

Alicia

I laid in bed and cried. She saw right through my façade and genuinely cared for me. She encouraged me to want to change and let go of the hurt I was feeling the pain. I told myself that I would change. I pushed the poured the bottles down the drain. I told myself I would not have sex with anyone else and I wouldn't compromise myself anymore.

That semester I did just that. I kept a low profile, and I made up with Zelle and Tiana. I didn't tell them exactly what was going on. I just told them I hadn't been myself for a while. I skipped out on the favorites dance this year, but it's okay I told myself I would try new things this year, I tried out for flashes. I also talked to the coach and would be playing basketball again next year and tried out for the dance team. I got my grades back up; life was starting to turn around. At the end of the year, the school decided to take us students to Six Flags. Mr. Bruno hooked Zelle and me up with free tickets. Zelle and I rode the bus together on the way to six flags. We talked about all the rides we wanted to get on.

"Hey who is that?", Zelle asked.

"I think his name is Jason," I said, "He is a new kid here."

"He is fine," she said.

"Yeah, I guess." He was attractive, but I wasn't looking to be involved with anyone. I wanted to focus on myself.

"Do you think he has a girlfriend?", she asked.

"I don't know," I said.

She rambled on about him for a little while. I stared out the window until I eventually fell asleep. The bus came to a stop, we had arrived. We got off the bus, and the teachers let us know the times we needed to meet back up. We walked around the park riding whichever rides we came to. My favorite was Catman. When it came to getting on Spluperman, I was not doing it. It consisted of seats where your legs would dangle. It took you up 300 feet and dropped you. Zelle wanted to ride it, but I didn't. I was going to wait on Zelle to get off until a classmate, Lynne asked me to ride shockwave with her. We walked over, there was no line. As we were getting on the ride, I turned to put my bag in a cubby, Chris sat in my seat so he could ride with Lynne. I didn't want to be an asshole, so I sat behind them. On the inside, I was freaking out. I had never ridden this ride before. I saw someone walking by, I grabbed them.

"Hey, can you ride this with me?" It was Jason.

He looked down at me, "Yeah."

"Thanks, I was freaking out I didn't want to ride alone," I said.

"No problem," he said.

After the ride, I thanked Jason again and went to find Zelle. We walked into this burger place to get food. Jason and

Chris walked in shortly after. As we sat down, they sat down with us.

"Can I have some? ", Jason asked.

"Umm, yeah, sure," Zelle said with a smile.

I shook my head and laughed. She was blushing so hard. After we ate, it was time to get back on the bus.

"Ke, do me a favor," Zelle said.

"What?"

"Hook me up with Jason," she said.

"You can't hook yourself up?", I asked.

"No, you know I get shy. Please!!!"

"Alright, alright," I said.

I asked Jason for his phone number as we were getting off the bus. I would can him later and try to hook him and Zelle up. After all, what were best friends for?

Jason

After I got home, I called Jason with Zelle on three-way. I facilitated the conversation but was there overall to help them talk, until Zelle had to get off the phone.

"I gotta go yall. Bye Jason", Zelle said.

"Bye." I clicked over to clear the line.

"Well Jason you know Zelle likes you, do you want to go out with her?", I said.

"She cool, but I kind of have my eye on somebody," he said.

"Oh, okay."

"It's you," he said.

"Me?" Oh crap. This is not going to end well. During my dark phase, I had slept with my friends' boyfriends/ crushes. I did not want to go back to that. "This that is going to work I don't want to hurt Zelle," I said.

"But what about what you want?", he said.

"I don't know you."

"Well get to know me," he said.

I had to admit I was a little interested. "Okay, so you want to come over tomorrow for a get-together?", I asked.

"Yeah, sure," he said.

I gave him my address and said goodbye. Tomorrow I would invite Zelle as well so they could hang out. Maybe if he got to know her, he would not be eyeing me. The next morning, I told Zelle about the plan.

"I can't come," Zelle said.

"What? Why not?"

"My mom is taking me to Breontay's, it's her birthday," she replied.

"Oh okay, I will cancel."

We hung up the phone, I tried to reach Jason, but he did not answer. At 8pm, he called and told me he was outside. I went to the door to let him in. We sat on the couch and played a racing game. We talked a bit about where he had come from and why he moved here. After the game, we put on a movie. He put his arm around me. I moved over to put more space in between us, but he followed. As the film went on his actions did as well. He slid his hands into my pants and started to finger me. I had not had sex with anyone in about six months. I wanted to push him away, but it felt good. Beyond my better judgment, I pulled his fingers out of me and dragged him to my bedroom. I took off his shirt, he pulled down my pants. Next thing I know we are in a full-on sex session. He rotated me into all these different positions I have never experienced. He made me scream louder than anyone had before. The strokes got deeper and faster, and my body shook. This was the first time I had cum since Niya, and my first time with a guy. Afterward, he didn't leave we laid there and fell asleep. That morning I helped him out of the window. I'm sure my mom was home from the club by now. I had enjoyed myself, but I felt guilty. How was I supposed to explain this to Zelle?

"Ke, where you able to cancel it?", she asked.

"Yeah, but we ended up talking on the phone," I said.

"What he say?"

I took a deep breath. "He says you are cool, but he likes me." I waited for her to curse me out before I said anything else.

"Oh, well you should give him a chance," she said.

I could tell she was bummed. "Are you sure? I don't want to mess up our friendship."

"Naw its good, plus Breontay is trying to hook me up with one of her classmates since I will be here for the summer," she replied.

"Look at you, on to the next like it ain't nothing."

She laughed, "yeah, well I gotta go, we supposed to be headed to the pool in a few."

"Alright, have fun!"

I know lying is wrong, but it was the only way not to hurt my friend. Plus, what she didn't know would not hurt her.

That summer Jason and I grew closer and closer. If he was sneaking over through to see me, we were on the phone. For my birthday, my mom took me to Ta' Tolly's for dinner. I invited Jason so he could meet my family. He bought me a bear and a card. My family gave interrogated him, but he was respectful, sweet and kind. He answered their questions as politely as he could. My family was pleased. However, I didn't trust him as far as I could throw him. He was handsome and always knew what to say. However, sometimes after I fucked him to sleep, I would look through his phone and see messages between him and other girls. He always had some excuse. Somebody was using his phone, she is just a friend, etc. I got into so many fights trying to keep what I thought was my happiness it was crazy.

One Saturday My mom had to work due to one of her employees calling off.

(Bing)

It was a picture text from my mom. Jason and some skinny bitch. I had to look at it a few times. I called me, she gave me all the details. He took some girl to my mom job as a date. I didn't even trip. I called up Brittney, and we went out to the party in Commerce. I was done crying and fighting over someone who apparently did not want to be with me.

Brittney and I walked in hyped. I grabbed a liquor slushy to help me get in the mood. I was twerking, busting splits and showing my ass in a circle, all that. Afterward, I made out with Trey.

(Ring)

"What the fuck you doing at the party?", he asked.

I hung up and sent the picture.

He blew my phone up, but I wouldn't answer until after I came.

He tried to explain, but I hung up and turned my phone off. The rest of the weekend I packed everything he gave me and burned it.

That Monday, Jason had several of his friends give me gifts, flowers cards, notes, and candy. He caught up with me in the halls and begged me to talk to him. We skipped the rest of our classes and walked to my house.

"The only reason I was with Ashley was that she piqued my curiosity. I had never met her before, but she knew a lot about me. I took her to your mom's job on purpose, so she could be a witness nothing happened", he explained.

"That what stupid, all you did was embarrass me," I said.

"I didn't mean to. I am sorry," he said. He grabbed my hands and fell to his knees. He looked up at me. "Please forgive me, it will not happen again."

I just stared at him. The smart part of me said to run like hell, but the stupid part of me did not want to. Okay. The dummy wins again. Plus, I was guilty myself. I didn't tell him about Trey. He lived in Dallas, and there was no way our paths should cross again.

We walked the rest of the way hand in hand. We got in, and I put my stuff down on the bed. I turned around, and he already had his shirt off.

"Oh no babe, we can't, I am on my period," I said.

"So...."

I looked at him like he was crazy. I always heard you were not supposed to have sex on your period. I am guessing because it was just gross. He pushed me down on the bed and pulled my pants off, makeup sex was the best.

Jason dang near lived with me after we made up. After school, he would come to my house and sneak in my window. My mom was not home much, and when she was, she was too preoccupied to know he was there with me, plus always had my door locked so I could hide him when she came in. We would complete our school work, watch tv, and make out. I would sneak him in food from dinner so he could eat. My bedroom was next to the bathroom, when everyone went to bed, we would shower and sleep. In the mornings he would leave early enough to go to change and catch the bus from his house. This lasted for three months.

One day I arrived at school and Jason wasn't there. I texted and called, but his phone was off. A few weeks went by, and I had not heard from him. I reached out to one of his cousins. Turns out he had moved back to Arkansas. His mom wanted to return to their hometown to help a sick family member. I could not believe this, every time I get close to someone, they are ripped away from me. I felt like God was doing this on purpose. I was down for a while, I stopped hanging with friends, and I just laid in the dark and listened to love songs while I cried.

Trapped in the Dark

I began acting out at school, or at least that what the counselors would tell my mom. Any and every little thing irked my nerves. I slapped a classmate for knocking my pen off my desk. I talked back to my basketball coaches and the leader of my group in dance. I was ditching school and drove to Commerce to beat Ashley's ass. I found out her location from Dajia. She always knew the scoop.

My flash director noticed my behaviors she was also friends with the dance teacher at the commerce school who saw me on tape. She called me into her office.

"Where were you yesterday at twelve?", she asked.

"I went to lunch," I said.

"Were you in Commerce?"

"No," I replied.

"I have a tape of you sneaking into the commerce school."

"I---"

"Do not lie to me. What's going on with you?"

I looked her in her eyes, then looked down. "I think I am pregnant," I said.

"What?"

"I think I am pregnant. I missed my period last month", I said.

"Have you told your grandmother?", she asked. Mrs. Davis and my granny were old friends. My Aunt Tiffaney was a dancer. She was the reason I became a dancer.

"No, mam. I really do not know how to.", I said.

I burst into tears. She gave me hug and let me cry in her shoulder. Then she called my grandmother since they were friends and helped me explain my situation. After the call, she told me my options, mostly about abortion. My granny picked me up, and we went to the free clinic. Sure, enough I was six weeks pregnant. I was in shock. I knew it was a possibility, but as reality started to seek in, I began to panic, I was pregnant with someone's child that I hadn't heard from in about a month. I walked back to the waiting room.

"Granny, I am six weeks pregnant," I said

She sighed, disappointment was all over her face. First my mom, now me. The curse of teen pregnancy was still standing strong in our family. "Do you want to keep it? It's early, you still have options."

"Yeah, I am," I said.

"Okay, I guess we will figure it out," she said.

The next day my mom took me to the health and human service department to apply for medical benefits. I was going to need it to help with all the medical appointments I would now require. As soon as the elevator door opened to the third floor. Reese from school was standing there. She looked at me.

"What are you doing here?", she asked.

"She pregnant! I am going to be a glam-ma!", my mom said.

I froze, this girl was not my friend, and now she was going to tell all my business before I had a chance to tell anyone myself. I was so angry with my mother. We walked out of the elevator as Reese got in. I turned to glimpse at her before the doors closed, she was texting. I knew tomorrow was going to be a terrible school day. After the office visit,

I received multiple calls from my friends. They knew already, I just confirmed the rumors. I muted my phone for the rest of the day and slept.

The next day at school I confirmed the results of the test to my dance directors. They just hugged me. It wasn't a congratulations hug, it was more like a hug as if someone just died, one you would give while mourning. After the hugs, they informed me that I could no longer be a part of the dance group. I understood, who wants to endorse a teen mom. I cleaned out my dance locker and apologized to my dance leader.

She hugged me. "It's okay, and if you need any help with that baby, you let me know."

"Okay," I said with a smile.

Not only was I kicked out of dance, but I was also kicked out of basketball. Everywhere I went there was always a group watching and whispering. I could try to avoid people, and it seems like there was always someone around staring at me. It wasn't just the kids. My teachers would look at me in disappointment. Some of them were slick with their insult's others were just all out rude, especially my health teacher. She was always saying I needed to learn this or that, and behave a certain way since I was having a baby. The worse thing was the rumors of who my baby's father was. Some thought it was Micah, others thought it was Trey's. I knew who's it was Jason, the guy who left me.

Each day it became harder and harder to show up at school and push through. My thoughts got darker and darker. I went to church thinking it would help and bring me some peace. I was headed to the back pew.

"Kennadi," sister Whelks was approaching me. She was the church mother.

"Yes," I said.

"I hear you are pregnant, is this true?"

"Yes, mam I ----" I didn't even finish my sentence.

"You stupid, stupid girl," she said.

My smile faded

She grabbed my hands. "I will pray for you, but your life is over." She threw my hands down and walked away.

I took a seat, my eyes filled with tears. She wasn't the only one telling me that. My mom's new boyfriend Tyson told me the same thing. I was at home from school due to not feeling well. He walked in the house in a hurry.

"Your mom tells me you are pregnant," he said.

"Yeah, I am"

"You know your life is over. You can't do anything anymore", he said.

I looked down and said nothing

"Break down this weed, I will give you $20. You gone need it for diapers anyway", he said.

I sat down at the table and began pulling the weed from the stems and put it in a bag. Tyson laid the twenty bucks on the table grabbed his bag and headed out the door.

I snapped back into the present, I had no idea what the preacher was talking about, I just wanted church to be over. I got home and cried. I couldn't take it anymore. I had lost my friends. At first, they would call to check on me. I thought it was sweet until they called just to throw in my face what they were doing. So, I stopped answering. Plus, most of their moms did not want them hanging out with the pregnant girl. My so-called best friend Tiana started talking about me. She told Zelle that I would be nothing, I would be stuck in Blueville my whole life and had no sense of direction. I couldn't go anywhere without being belittled or fussed at. I knew I had messed up. I didn't need to hear it every time I walked out the door. I wrote a note to my mom:

Dear Mom,

I can't do this anymore. I tried my best to deal with things. From the loss of my father family and friends. Now I am a pregnant teenager. Everyone is always talking about me and yelling at me. I try to push through, but the thoughts in my head are too hard to carry. The demons in my mind are winning. I love you guys. But I don't want to be here anymore. Maybe things will be different with my father.

Ke

I laid it on her bed. I figured she would get it when she got home from the store. I walked into the kitchen and found the biggest knife in the drawer. I went into the bathroom and sat on the floor. I pressed the blade against my chest and cried. I wanted to die. I knew suicide was a sin but having a child out of wedlock was as well. If I killed myself would it be just suicide or suicide and homicide in God's eyes? My thoughts were not straight. I dropped the knife and cried for a while then picked up the knife again. I heard my mom come in the door.

"Ke, help me with the groceries. Ke?!?"

I closed my eyes holding the knife to my chest. A few moments later my mom pushed into the bathroom and snatched the knife and threw it. She looked me in the eyes and just hugged me. I squeezed her back, and I just laid there and cried into her shoulder as she sobbed into mine. Minutes passed, and we got ourselves together.

"Kennadi, if you were struggling this bad, why didn't you let me know," she said.

"When was I supposed to? You were so happy to have a grandchild. I didn't want to bring you down."

"Don't worry about me. I am the parent it is my job to take care of you. Suicide is selfish. Do you know how many people care about you? What about your brother? How do you think he would feel?", she asked.

I started to cry again. "See you are worried about how everyone else feels. What about me?", I screamed.

I pushed past her and ran into my room and locked the door. She knocked on it for a while, then silence. I guess she had given up. At my next doctors' appointment, my mom discussed my suicide attempt to my gynecologist. They had me fill out a survey and told me to be honest. The results showed I was severely depressed. She recommended that I go to Mary's Manor, a behavioral health hospital to be evaluated. We were to head over there after the appointment.

Mary's Manor was a behavioral health/ mental health hospital. Most of us just called it the crazy house and avoided it at all cost. It was a large brick building located on the edge of town. As soon as we walked in, I heard screams and moans, a girl was in the waiting room with cuts up her wrist was rocking back and forth, other kids were being restrained. Oh, hell no was what I was thinking. I was down, but I wasn't staying here. I pulled myself together. The evaluator came and got me. She asked me many of the same questions that were on the depression survey, this time I changed all the answers. I said everything with a smile and just told her I was feeling a little stressed due to the pregnancy. We walked back to the waiting room.

"Ms. Williams, she is fine. Just a little overwhelmed with the pregnancy. Nothing serious enough to have her here", the doctor said.

"Okay, thank you!"

My mom and I got up to leave when we heard more screaming. We dang near ran to the car. I knew from then on out I was going to hide my depression, I did not want to end up in that hospital. On the way home, we stopped by Jack in the Crack for dinner. My phone went off

"Hey, what you doing?"

It was Jason. I had not heard from this guy in about two months. "Nothing about to eat you?"

"Nothing I am in town, you mind if I come over later?", he asked.

"No, come at 9pm", I said.

I hung up the phone as my mom approached the car. She went on talking about how it is essential to keep my stress level down, the baby, and baby names. After dinner, I showered and listened to music. I tried to figure out how exactly I was going to tell Jason I was pregnant.

(Tap tap)

I went to the window, it was Jason. He climbed in, "Hey babe as he approached me."

"I don't want no stupid hug. Where the hell have you been? You don't know how to call or text somebody?", I said.

"I am sorry we had to move."

"Why? Your mom couldn't move and go help her sister by herself?"

"My mom told everyone we had to move to help Aunt Macie, but the truth is she couldn't afford to keep the house anymore after she was fired from her job," he said.

"Really?", I am sorry. "Where is your dad?"

"He has been in jail for the last ten years. You know, I have ten brothers and sisters. My mom started struggling, and we needed help. We moved in with aunt Macie. My phone was off because I couldn't pay it anymore. Not until I started mowing lawns. I thought about you the whole time", he said.

I smiled, "I need to tell you something. I---"

"I know about your dad. Your grandmother told me. She warned me to keep an eye on you, so I wouldn't end up like her son, your dad", he said.

"I---" Tears filled my eyes, "I would never hurt you."

He kissed my forehead, "I know and wrapped his arms around me."

"I need to tell you something. I am pregnant."

"What?"

"Yeah, two months pregnant," I said.

"Are you serious?"

"Yeah," he laid his hand on my stomach.

(Silence)

"I know this is a lot. You do not have to stay around if you do not want to", I said. He was a great athlete, he had a scholarship Florida state lined up. I didn't want to destroy his life.

"I am not going anywhere," he said.

After we messed around, we cuddled and drifted off to sleep. The next morning, I woke up he was gone. There was a note on my pillow. He had to leave town with his mom this morning. I got up for breakfast. Jason had texted me multiple times to check on me. He called and texted daily, and whenever he was in town, he would drop by. I was happy he was back in the picture.

Time passed, and I got bigger. I found out a few weeks ago that I was having a boy. Jason was excited, he wanted a Jayden. Jayden was causing my back so much pain. My body started to hurt everywhere and walking long distances in school was killing me. So many stairs. After class one day I decided to eat lunch in the gym. I sat down with Lori, a girl I played basketball with. Zelle walked in later she came and sat down beside Lori. No one said anything for a while.

"Are you going to Jam the Gym?", Lori asked.

"Yeah," Zelle said

"Sweaty boys and balls, that's why I'm in this position," I said, "Naw I ain't going." They burst out laughing.

"Ke I am sorry I haven't been there for you, My mom---"

"It's cool," I understand.

We started talking about senior year. School would be out soon, and we would be off to College, or at least they would be.

"Ohhh!"

"What's wrong with you?", asked Lori.

"Something's wrong," I said.

I buckled down. "Loriiii," I screamed. She grabbed my hand, and I squeezed. "Help me to the nurse!"

They both grabbed an arm and got me to the nurse's office. I was transported to the hospital shortly after. Turns out I was in premature labor. The doctors gave me medicine to stop the contractions. They were going to keep me a few days. They also gave me steroids to boost my son's lung development to increase the chances of him having mature lungs if born early. Eventually, the labor stopped, and I could go home. My mom told me on the way home the school had called, and I had to remain homebound until after the baby arrived. I hated this. I was already isolated at school, and now I would be stuck at home with no one, only visit from my homebound teacher once a week to help me keep up with my assignments.

Teen Mom

My due date was getting closer, and my mom wanted to have a baby shower. She said my God-Mom wanted to host. This was a shock. My God-mom had basically disowned me since finding out I was pregnant.

"Is it okay if Jason and his family come?", I asked.

She eyed me for a while. "I guess."

My mom hated Jason, she thought he was no good for me. I hoped she would get over that, we were having a child together, and I was going to need him and her to help me when Jayden arrived. However, Jason's family wasn't very fond of me either. They were a churchgoing bunch. They believed women should only wear skirts and long sleeve shirts. I once went to dinner at their house. They sent a 3-year-old to tell me to pull up my shirt. I guess it didn't help that when I did first meet them, I was four months pregnant. From that point on I made sure to dress appropriately around them, I wanted to keep the peace between us. I wanted my child to know both sides of his family.

 The day of the baby shower arrived quickly. Jason, his mom, and sisters came first. I tried to introduce them to my mom. She gave a half smile and went to greet the next guest. I apologized for her and showed Jason's family to their seats. More people pilled in beside Zelle and Brittney, most people there were family and my mom's friends. We ate, played games, and socialized. My god-mom had made a cake a little baby boy was laying on a sunflower, it was so cute. Then I opened gifts and thanked everyone for showing. Jason and I went outside to talk. His family was staying at a hotel in town. He wanted to stay a little longer to help me put up the gifts afterward. My mom wasn't too excited about him being around, but she let him stay. We put the presents up and watched a movie. As I was hanging up his clothes.

(Pop) (Splash)

My water broke. I ran to the bathroom to check. There was amniotic fluid everywhere.

"Jason!"

He walked to the bathroom. "Ms. Kassie!!!", he yelled as he ran out to get my mom.

I got my hospital bag and headed to the car. On the way, Jason called his mom and let them know to meet us at the hospital. My labor was quick about four hours long. Jayden arrived with no problem. Jason recorded the birth and mom took pictures.

(Chaos)

Doctors were scrambling, bells were ringing, my mom and Jason were pushed out of the room. I passed out. I woke in another room. Jason was sitting in a chair across from me.

"Where is Jayden? Where is my baby?", I said as I looked around.

"He is being transported, he, he couldn't breathe," he said.

I was I'm shock, I wanted to move, but my body was still numb from the epidural I couldn't do anything but cry.

(Knock)

"Would you like to see your son?", a nurse said.

"Yes," I said.

She rolled in a gurney with my son in an incubator. He had tubes coming out of everywhere I couldn't look. I was so sad and mad at the same time. My baby was here, and I couldn't hold him or touch him. Jason walked up to the incubator and touched it.

"We are sending him to Children's Medical," the nurse said. A few minutes later she rolled him away.

"Ke, I am going to children's with Jayden I will call you with updates," my mom said as she ran in and back out of the door.

Jason's Mom came in, brought me pizza, and kissed my forehead. They would have to leave, but she would leave Jason behind. He was going to stay at his aunt's house for the week, so he could be close.

A couple of days passed, and I could be released from the hospital. My mom came and got Jason and me and drove us straight to Children's. When I arrived, they told me I could be able to stay in a room down the hall from the NICU. I had to be there for two weeks, Jayden would be ready to leave then. I walked into the room. He was no longer in the incubator, he was breathing on his own.

"You want to hold him," a nurse asked.

I picked him up, and he held my finger. I was in love and grateful, my baby boy had made it. They would allow me to take Jayden to our room. This is where things took a turn. My mom was there as well she complained about everything I did. You are holding him wrong, wipe his mouth, hold his head, etc. Every time Jason would pick up Jayden she would come over and take him. I knew she was trying to help, but she was causing issues. Jason felt like he couldn't be a parent to his own son, and I was tired of the complaints. Even when we went to sleep, it was more nagging. You should sleep in the bed Jason should sleep in the chair, yall shouldn't be hugged up here. My stress level started to rise. I couldn't even do right by my child anymore, I struggled. A nurse came in one day when I was crying, I couldn't get Jayden to eat, and his weight was dropping.

"You need to get this down," the nurse said.

"I know I am trying," I said.

"Not enough."

I gave Jayden to Jason.

"You need to learn yourself. You are not doing this right you are going to need a lot of help", she said as she left the room.

"You know what, fuck this, Jason when we leave, you take Jayden with you. I can't do this", I yelled. It was bad enough everyone was telling me my life was over, my mom was nagging me, and now this nurse was downing me. I was sick of it.

"Kennadi this is your child," my mom said.

"It's his too!"

"You are being a bad mother," she said.

"Well I learned from the best," I said. How could she complain about my parenting skills? Did she forget her actions? Did she forget I grew up with my granny, not her? The nights I took care of her as she stumbled into the house after a night of partying. The fact that she was too busy living her own life, she rarely had time for us.

Silence filled the room. My mom grabbed her stuff and left.

Later that night I got a text from my brother.

Ke you and your dude bet not ever say anything else to make my mother cry.

I didn't even reply. He did not even know the situation, and honestly, I was too mentally drained to get into an argument with anyone else today. Due to Jayden losing weight rapidly he no longer could stay in the room with us. I had to wake up every three hours, walk down the hall to the NICU and feed him. They made me do this to prove I would do what was needed to take care of him when it was time to take him home. I couldn't help but feel some type of way, but I did what was needed to be done so we could leave this place.

Time had come for us to be released from the hospital. My granny came and got us. When we arrived at the house. Jason mom was there waiting. School was going to start soon, and Jason had to go home. At the hospital, we planned for Jason to come to get Jayden every other weekend after he was two months old. We hugged goodbye, and he kissed Jayden's forehead. I walked into the house my mom was waiting. She hugged Jayden then helped us into the house. I wanted to talk about the argument, but she avoided the conversation. That's pretty much how it goes in this household. When there is a problem, sweep it under the rug.

Graduation and a Wedding

Thanks to the help of some government programs, I was able to pay a babysitter so I could finish high school and get formula for my baby. Feeding a baby without a job was hard. I applied to many places, but I kept getting turned down for lack of experience. I needed work, but I was really just happy I could go back to school, I did not want to be a teen mom and a dropout, and I was sick and tired of my mom complaining about what she was doing for us, meanwhile telling me I needed to go to school. Education was highly valued in my family when compared to finding a job, my folks believe education was the key to getting out of the hood. School was a break from my responsibilities. Even though I had my baby, people were still gossiping. The only friend I had left was Zelle. I didn't care, with all my responsibilities I had no time to hang out anyway. Senior year I would just keep my head down and focus on my grades so that I could graduate, do something right.

In a few weeks, Jayden would be two months old. It was time for his first trip with his dad. I started packing up Jayden bag. I was excited about the break. I could get a dearly start on my project, and I was happy Jason and Jayden would have some time to bond.

"What are you doing," my mom said.

"Jason is coming to get Jayden," I replied.

"What? Why?"

"Well he is his dad," I said.

"You going?"

"No, I'm going to work on my history project," I said.

She had a digested look on her face.

"What?", I asked.

"What kind of mom ships their child off unsupervised?"

"He will be with his dad," I said.

"Whatever, I ought to call CPS on you. A Terrible mother she said as she slammed the door."

I continued packing, I had gotten used to my moms' insults. I tried to ignore them and remain calm she was supporting us. That weekend I stayed in my room mostly, I would clean up when my mom was gone and hide out when she was home. Sunday afternoon Jason returned with Jayden.

"We need to talk," he said.

"About?"

"Well I am thinking of going to the Navy," he said.

"What? Why?"

"I feel like it's the only way we will be able to live together as a family. These trips back and forth are getting old. Your mom hates me, and it is getting harder to deal with", he said.

I could understand that. I was also sick of dealing with my mom mood swings, but I didn't want him to go. "My uncle was in the air force, and I never saw him."

"Look I know it's going to be hard at first, but I think it will be worth it," he said.

"Yeah… Alright. I think you should go", I said. I guess he could tell I didn't mean it.

He lifted my head. "We will only be apart for a little while, I promise."

Senior year was ending. Graduation was next week, and it was bittersweet. I would graduate, but my love would be going to boot camp. We would have no contact for weeks, after that he was slated to go to school for four more months.

Even though Jason was somewhat out of the picture, the relationship between my mother and me got worse.

"Who drank all the Dr. Pidds?"

I heard her storming through the house.

"Kennadi did you drink all the sodas?"

"No," I said. I bet Marq did. He was always having company over and giving out our snacks to everyone.

"Girl drop the attitude."

"I---"

"You make me sick walking around her with an attitude like you pay the bills. If it weren't for my grandson, I would put your ungrateful fast ass out", she yelled.

I got up and packed started packing Jayden diaper bag

"Where the fuck do you think you are going?", she asked.

"To aunt Tiff's," I said. Tiff lived around the corner from us now.

She snatched the bag.

"Look ma I don't want to argue with you today," I said.

(Clap) She slapped me across the face.

I turned around and picked up Jayden. I walked towards the door, and she blocked it. I pushed her, so hard that she fell into the door behind her and hit the floor. She looked up at me in shock. I picked up Jayden's bag and walked out of the door. When I arrived at my aunt's house, I explained to her what happened. She offered to let me, and Jayden stay in her back room until things were to cool down between my mom and me. In the meantime, I went to school, took care of Jayden, and wrote Jason each day. I had started community college to earn my medical coding and billing certificate. My granny worked as a coder and could help me get a job at the hospital.

After Jason was out of boot camp, he bought a ticket to fly to Maine. I flew there where I would come and see him. I didn't want to take Jayden on a flight this young, so I left him with my grandmother. My Aunt Tiffaney and Aunt Diana took the trip with me. It was my first time flying, and I wasn't going alone. The lines at the airport were ridiculous. When we finally got on the plane, I was so sleepy. The pilot came on, he discussed us taking off and the emergency landing information. The attendants passed out brochures. Looking at those things freaked me out I wanted to run off that plane, but the doors were sealed. The aircraft began to move we were about to take off. As we approached the runway, my stomach dropped. I pulled down the window covering and laid my head on the dinner stand. Lord, please let us make it I thought. I closed my eyes and laid on that table the whole flight, repeating that same sentence.

When we landed, we took a rental to get to the hotel Jason ad reserved from us. My aunts dropped me off and headed to their room. I knocked on the room number Jason gave me. He had balloons, rose petals, and candles everywhere. On the table was a heart-shaped pizza, our favorite drinks, and cupcakes. I dropped my bags on the floor and jumped onto him; we had sex. Afterward, we went to take a shower. We got out and dried off. He left the bathroom as I washed my face. I turned to walk out of the bathroom

"Kennadi I think you left the water on," he said.

I went to go check when I came back out Jason was on one knee.

"Kennadi Venay Williams, will you marry me?", he asked.

I stood there with my hands covering my gapped mouth. I nodded my head, yes, and he slid the ring on my finger. It had a large diamond in the middle the band consisted of a white gold band with a row of smaller diamonds in the center. I ran to the door.

"Where are you going?", he asked.

"To show my aunts!"

"You may want to put on some clothes first," he said.

"Right!"

I got dressed and ran over to share the news. My aunts were excited for me. We jumped up and down, and they took a picture to share the ring back at home. I ran back over to the room. We ate dinner watched movies and made love again. I was only there for a weekend, but Jason was determined to show me as much as he could. We ate at all these different restaurants, checked out museums, and took me to the casino.

It had been two months since I had seen Jason, but we talked every day. Jayden was beginning to put words together as well. Jason would be coming in town soon, and we were going to have our Wedding, this way the next place he moved to, Jayden and I could go as well. My granny and aunt helped me pay for my wedding dress. I choose a white A-line gown with red trim my bridesmaids wore red to match my dress. Jason wore his uniform. My cousin Mary made all the decorations, and I created the invitations and wedding programs. By the time Jason would arrive everything was good to go.

I still felt a little incomplete. I had invited my grandma Jean and Kaydence, but they had not RSVP'd yet. My dad would not be able to walk me down the aisle, but I wanted some part of him to be there. The wedding came together well given the amount of time we had. It was a small wedding, but both of our families were present. Jean and Kaydence did not show, but my dad's aunt and her daughter did, which meant a lot to me. I was so giddy, I never thought I would be getting married. Growing up I did not want to be married, no one in my family was, and if they were, it failed. At the reception, my mom pulled me aside. We really had not been seeing eye to eye, I hope she was not about to fuss at me on my wedding day.

"Kennadi I know I haven't been the best mom. I treated Jason the way I did because I was afraid, he would take yall away from me", she said.

"Mom he is not taking me away. I will still come and visit."

"I know I just didn't want you to go, but I see now that he really does love yall. I just want you to be happy", she said. She hugged me tight and wiped the tears from her eyes.

"I am happy," I said and hugged her back.

After the wedding night, we went to spend time with his side of the family because he was leaving soon. While I was away, Jean told me why she did not come, she didn't want to see another man, who wasn't her son walk me down the aisle. I could understand, but it hurt. She could've walked me down the aisle in his place. I told her it was okay, I didn't want her to feel bad, and I didn't want this situation to distract me from the time I had with my husband. It was soon time to drop Jason off at the airport, he had to report to his duty station soon. I wasn't sad this time, because in two weeks I would be there with him. We were moving to Virginia. To help us start off, my grandmother gave us the chair and couch from her house to put in the living room and a dining table. My mom allowed me to take my entire bedroom set. Jason had already bought Jayden a car shaped bed. We had received dishes, silverware, and other essentials as gifts from the wedding, so we had an excellent start to our apartment. The only thing left to do was say goodbye. My immediate family met at my mom's house we hugged and wished each other well. My mom drove me to Zelle's. Walking to the door, it all started to hit. This would be the last time I walked to this door. I knocked, Zelle opened it.

"Hey honey, I just wanted to come to say goodbye."

"You are really leaving," she said.

I nodded my head. I couldn't speak due to the lump in my throat. How do you say goodbye to your best friend wrapped my arms around her and we both squeezed. I smiled with tears running down my face and turned to walk out. I got into the car, as we pulled away all I saw was Zelle standing in the door was tears in her eyes and waving goodbye.

Changes

The trip to Virginia was long. We took many backroads and got lost in the hood of Georgia. Jayden was so tired of being in that car seat. He got so mad, he repeatedly splashed us with juice, like a preacher throwing holy water on a Sunday. Finally, we had arrived, and the journey was over. We arrived at the resident office. After being cared and explaining who I was, I received the key to the apartment. Jason was underway, so I wove must move into our apartment before him. It was a small little place, two bedrooms and a bathroom, but it was perfect for my little family. My mom stayed for a few days but would have to return to Texas for work. She took me grocery shopping before she left. She hugged Jayden and me goodbye and headed out the door. As she shut the door, I saw the tears in her eyes, our relationship was not perfect, but we still had love for each other. I got an email from Jason:

I was supposed to come in, but since there is a hurricane coming, we must stay out until it passes.

Hurricane? I didn't know there was a hurricane coming. We didn't have cable yet. I had been watching a movie I downloaded to a thumb drive. I went to the front office to get information about hurricanes and what I should have; they printed off a list. I had seen the dollar store and walked to it. I bought candles and went to buy flashlights, batteries, and candles. I had the other necessities form my mom taking me grocery shopping. The storm would come, the power was out for three days, and the street had flooded bad, but we made it through.

That afternoon Jason arrived home. Jayden ran to him and grabbed his leg as I grabbed his upper body. Finally, our little family was together. We had our own place, and we were bonding as a family. After a few months, things started to change. Jason became distant, he was never at home he was either at work out with his friends. Sometimes he would come in at two in the morning. His excuse was always he was the designated driver. I knew better. As I was doing laundry, I would find pieces of paper with random phone numbers on them. I had asked him about the numbers in the past, but he said he only took them not to be rude. I didn't believe him, but since things were rocky, I did not want to make matters worse with my insecurities. There were so many nights I had cried myself to sleep, waiting for him to return home to me. What was I supposed to do? I had finally made it out of Blueville, I needed this fresh start, I wanted to escape my past. Plus, Jason took care of me, he wasn't perfect, but he was a good man.

Tonight, was date night. I made steaks, topped with shrimp, potatoes, and fresh green beans. Hours had passed. Where is he, I thought, it was 9pm.

"Jason are you cheating on me?", I asked.

"What kind of dumb ass question is that?"

"Well you always gone, and you never want to do anything with us? I want to know why you are being distant", I said

"I go with my friends to escape!"

"Escape what?", I asked.

"Look my job is stressful and taking care of a family is hard. You just sit here all day. Why don't you work? You just look to me to take care of everything", he said.

"First of all, it's hard to find a job when you have no help. I have tried. We do not have any family to help us, we can't afford childcare, and I don't know anyone to watch our kid", I said wiping the tears from my eyes. You think I like sitting in this house all day?"

"I just want to be free sometimes. I didn't realize how much harder things would be after you guys got here", he said.

"Free? Okay!" I threw the dinner plates on the floor. "We can get our shit and leave," I said as I walked into the room. He quickly followed. He slapped me and threw me against the wall. He grabbed my shoulders

"You disrespectful bitch," he said while shaking my shoulders.

Jayden heard the commotion and ran into the room. Jason punched him in the face. I lost it I kicked him in the balls and ran to my son. I put Jayden in his room and shut the door. I turned around, and Jason grabbed my neck. He put so much pressure on my throat, I passed out.

"Mommy, Mommy!"

I woke to Jayden calling my name while trying to wake me. "Where is your dad?", I asked.

"Daddy went bye-bye," he said.

I looked around, and Jason was nowhere in sight. I got myself together and tucked Jayden into bed. I slept beside him and locked the door to the room. That morning I woke, I searched the house. Jason was nowhere to be found. I picked up the phone to call my mom.

"Hey Ke"

"I want to come home," I said sobbing.

"Why? What's wrong?"

"It's not working out between Jason and me. I---"

"Yall will be okay you just have to work it out," she said.

"But Mom---"

"Plus, where would you stay? I live with my boyfriend and granny house is full".

Apparently, tough times had fallen on my family. My brother cousins and aunt were living in my grandmother's house now.

"There is nothing good in Blueville for you," she added.

Someone was calling her in the background. "I have to go Ke."

(Dial tone)

Jason finally came home.

"I'm sorry I know I haven't been the husband you deserve. I should not have put my hands on you, or Jayden", he said.

"What is wrong with you?"

"To be honest, I think it is work. I hate it. I feel like I am property. Do this do that, report here. That's what I get every day", he said.

"But why do you take it out on us? We do nothing but love you", I said.

"I know, I messed up." He held his head.

I walked over to him and laid my hand on his shoulder.

Jayden peeked his head out of his room. "Mommy?"

"It's okay," I said. Jayden shut the door to his room.

"We can work this out," I said to Jason. "We just need a little help. There is a place on the base that will offer counsel for us."

He nodded his head.

Reaching Out

I made an appointment the next day. We attended counseling once a week for a month. That's all the time we had because Jason would have to do another underway. This one would be two months long. Dropping Jason off was terrible I would always cry. It always hurt to know you wouldn't see your significant other for a while. The first couple of weeks I stayed in the house. I still had not met anyone, I was so lonely. I went to the park and the beach to try and pass the time, but it did not help much. I was still alone.

One Saturday I was cleaning, and there was a knock on the door.

"Hi, my name is Charlene Wright. My husband and I have a church in Pembroke Circle. We would love to invite you to a service", she said. She then gave me a card.

"Oh, thank you," I said.

"Hope to see you soon," she said as she walked away.

I checked out the card. I may as well check them out tomorrow. This could be a good way for me to make friends, Jayden too. I know he was getting tired of looking at me every day.

I arrived at the church, it was in an office suite space. There was a small stage and chairs lined for guest to sit. It was only about fifteen people there, including kids. It was different from any church I had been to in Texas. Charlene greeted me, she then introduced me to her husband, the Pastor, and a few other members of the church. Everyone was kind and inviting, I was happy to be back in church. I always felt better when I went. I felt like I was starting the week off right. We're working out great, hanging with the ladies at church helped take my mind off my husband being gone. I attended the church weekly for a couple of weeks, but things started to change. They would ask me to come to hang out or fellowship in between services. I agreed. I felt like it would be a great way to pass the time as Jason was still away. We were meeting up at the beach.

"I love your swimsuit," said Ella

"Thanks, we are twins aren't we," I said. Our swimsuits matched.

We sat down to set up the picnic.

"Jayden do you want to play in the water?"

He nodded and ran over to play with Carlie's son. We continued to set up the picnic.

"Ahhhhhh! Momma!"

I turned around, and Jayden was running at me full speed. "What's wrong baby?", I asked.

"Jason threw a rock at me."

"Jason!", Carlie called her son over. "What happened?"

"I was just playing the rock didn't even hit him that hard," Jason said.

"Oh Okay," she replied.

I checked out Jaden to make sure he was okay. "Do you want to go back and play?"

"No," he said.

"Okay, sit right here."

"OMG, you are fine stop being a titty baby," Charlie said.

I turned my head to face her so quick I damn near had whiplash. "What did you just say?"

"He is being a titty baby, he needs to grow up," she said.

"First of all, my child is none of your concern, and you need to be concerned about your child and why he was throwing stuff in the first place. Teach him some home training", I said

The other ladies were just sitting there. They didn't say a word. I got our stuff and left. I was fuming. It took everything I had not to go across this bitch face. This wasn't the first time she rubbed me the wrong way. Last time, I was talking to Charlene and explaining why I was feeling so down. Carlie butted in saying I was just whining because my husband was gone, and I needed to get over it. I wanted to pop her in the mouth then, but I was trying to change, be more mature. I had been watching what I said and how I said it. Trying not to be so sensitive or go off on people because they offended me. My husband wanted me to change. He wanted me to dress and act like a military wife, and I was trying, I wanted our marriage to work. Acting crazy with church people was not a step in the right direction.

After this incident, I fell back. I still went to church, but that was it, until Easter.

"Sister Johnson, I noticed you haven't attended at any fellowships lately," said Pastor Wright.

"Yeah, I have been a little preoccupied. My husband will be home soon. I am trying to get things together for when he returns", I lied.

"Well, I want you to come over for Easter dinner. It will be at our home", he said.

"Okay," I said. I didn't really know how to say no to the pastor.

I arrived at their home. I walked into the house and dropped off the dishes I had brought. Last time there was a dinner it was a potluck, Ella called me out for not bringing anything, but I made sure I did this time. I spoke to everyone, except Carlie and found me a corner to sit in. After everyone arrived, we ate and then the children went up to play. The group was discussing gay marriage and how it was wrong how the bible was used in the wedding ceremonies for them. I just sat back and listened. What was I supposed to say? You know I was into girls before guys. However, they didn't know that. A few minutes later the pastor's son came running down the stairs crying.

"Jayden hit me," screamed Nate.

"It was an accident, Andre pushed me, and I fell on him," said Jayden.

"Well in this house if you can hit you get hit back," Pastor Wright said.

Before I knew it, he instructed his son to hit Jayden in the face. Jayden tried to run, but the pastor's other son grabbed him. Jayden started crying. I picked my son up and left. That was the last time they would see me. Churches were supposed to be a place you could go to be uplifted and lead in a positive direction. All these people did was criticize my lifestyle, my parenting, and destroy the little piece I had. I wanted to connect with people, but this was not working.

Jason finally returned. We had three weeks together before he would have to leave for deployment.

"Kennadi I was thinking, we should live with roommates," he said.

"I thought we discussed this before. I didn't want to live with anyone."

"My friend on the boat just moved his pregnant wife up, and I think it would be a good idea for yall to live together," he said.

"I don't know about that."

"We could save money, and you could get the new furniture you wanted," he said.

I thought about what was discussed at counseling. He always felt I was against him, and his ideas. I didn't want him to feel that way this time. "Okay," I said.

"I will set up a meet up for y'all since we have to do another underway," he said.

The under ways were becoming more and more frequent since they would have to go on deployment soon. That weekend there was a game between the members on the sub. Ryan and Imani came over. The guys decided to leave us at home to try to get to know one another. At first, it was awkward, but she seemed to be a cool chick. She was from Missouri. This was the first baby she had we shared stories about our past and experiences with the military lifestyle so far. Things were going well, so we decided to have a sleepover next month while the guys were away. Jason left for the underway. While he was gone, I enrolled Jayden into preschool and started my internship. I had started back going to school to finish my medical billing and coding diploma. All I had to do now was complete my internship portion course. Life with Imani was easy, she filled the loneliness I had felt since I had left Texas. I had tried to hang with other wives, but with her it was different. It was like we knew each other our entire lives. Us staying together definitely helped pass the time Jason was away.

It was time for deployment, and Imani would be moving in. Everything started out fine until she went into labor at twenty-four weeks. This was her first pregnancy, I couldn't imagine going through your first pregnancy without your husband.

"Kennadi!", she screamed.

"Yeah?"

"I'm bleeding," she said. She opened the door with her hand soaked.

"What?!? Okay!"

I woke my son, and we hopped in the car. I speed to the hospital. Turns out her amniotic sack was bulging from her cervix. They had to transport her to a specialty hospital. I called tiffany, and she met me at the hospital. I called our ombudsman and red cross to get a message to Ryan. As we waited for a response, I stayed at the hospital until things settled. They told us she was in early labor and would have to stay at the hospital until the baby came. She was so upset I tried to console her. I had her make a list of stuff she needed from home, and I went to go get them.

(Ring)

"Can you come back?", Imani asked. "I am having an emergency C-section tonight."

"What? Yeah, I am on the way."

By the time I got there she had already had the baby and was coming out of surgery. She was in good spirits, mostly high off the drugs. The next day we learned Isis would have to stay at the hospital because she was underweight. Imani cried I cried with her but informed her Isis was strong and that she may have to stay, but at least she was here. She was told that she did not qualify for housing at the hospital. I promised I would bring her to visit her as much as I could.

Things eventually took a turn for the worst Isis was okay, but Imani couldn't handle everything going on. She began smoking weed and drinking excessively. I tried to take her to the beach in between visits to see Isis, but she would be so drunk that by the time we got there she just slept. When we made it home, I would have to help her get out of the car and into the bed to sleep it off. There was also her turning cold. We were at the hospital seeing Isis when my mom called to tell me my grandfather was in the hospital. He had always had a bad heart, but it was getting worse. Only 14 percent of his heart was working.

"Imani, my grandpa in the hospital," I said. "It's not looking good."

"How old is he?", she asked.

"Sixty- Five, he has always had heart issues, but it is getting worse," I said as I wiped the tears from my eyes. I had lost my dad already. Losing my grandfather would be like losing my father all over again.

"Well, he has lived a long enough life," she said. Then she turned away and headed to the NICU.

I knew she had a lot going on, but she didn't have to be a bitch about it. I was the only person here trying to help her. I let it go. After weeks of her attitude, I complained to my husband via email, he thought I was overreacting. We began to argue a lot more. The rest of the deployment we basically argued over the situation he put me in. While Isis was gaining weight, other health issues were going on. Out of sympathy, I took Imani to the hospital more and more to verify she could be there for her baby. I eventually had to quit my internship to keep up with the restricted visiting hours at the hospital. I was exhausted, but at least the guys would be home soon.

The first couple of days were awkward everyone was trying to get used to each other again. Isis was able to come home right before the guys arrived, but this put pressure on Imani and Ryan. They argued a lot. One day it got so bad Ryan locked Imani out of their room. She just stood in the kitchen crying. I remembered how I felt when Jason and I argued like that, I went into the kitchen with her and hugged her as she cried. Things changed when babies were born, but they would be okay I thought. Jason and I were on good terms. The night he returned I planned a romantic night for us. He arrived home to a candlelit bedroom with roses everywhere. I put on some slow music, and we ate dinner. I cooked his favorite meal and massaged his entire body. They rolled him over and took care of that pent-up energy, it had been six months. It seemed we were revisiting our honeymoon stage.

After spending time with our child, we would stay up and just laugh and talk. I had my best friend back until the

Smiths problems began to rub off on us. We began to stay on edge all the time. Jason and I could barely stand to be around each other. Ryan had started drinking and staying out all night. When he was home, he was a drunken mess. I could not deal with this crap anymore I wanted them out. Since we still a little strapped for cash Jason was against this. A few more months had passed, and I was way over this situation. I was angry and more frustrated than I had been before. I was stressed out and couldn't keep anything down. I made a doctor's appointment, turns out I was pregnant. I cried, I wanted more kids, but not now, and I was not even sure I wanted them with Jason. Our marriage was a mess right now. I decided I wouldn't tell him until I was sure I wanted to keep it, and we could work things out.

I eventually made a Spacebook page to escape. It was a way for me to catch up with my old friends and avoid the negative situation I was living in. I wanted to change. I felt like the reason my life was so shitty was due to the way I treated people when I was younger. Karma really was a bitch. I connected with many of my classmates. I apologized to my half-sister for not being there for her, I apologized to my cousin that I convinced to have sex and she ended up pregnant, I reached out to fix my friendship with Tiana, and I apologized and made up with Rachel. I was cleaning my slate. I wanted to be a better me. A friend suggestion popped up, and I blushed. Darnell Stevenson, I clicked the add friend link. Since I was trying to clear up things, why not finally clear up things with him. A few minutes later he accepted the request.

Hey Best Friend, he wrote.

Hey what you been up to? I replied

The message board went on for a while, so I decided to move the conversation to the messenger.

I need to tell you something, I wrote.

What's up?

I don't know if you ever knew, but I used to be in love with you. If I heard your name, it made me smile. I am not sure if you ever felt that way, but I just wanted to let you know, I typed.

Call me

What's your number?

214-123-1234

I called after a few rings he picked up.

"Hello," he said.

My heart froze. That voice, that voice hasn't changed at all. "Hey, it's me."

"Kennadi?"

"Yeah It's been a while," I said.

"Yeah, 14 years."

We talked about a few events of the past and our current situations. He had a girl, and I was married.

"You had me in my feelings earlier. Why didn't you say anything before?", he asked.

"I didn't know what to say."

"Well, I loved you too. You were the reason I never kept any girlfriends. It was obvious."

"Not to me, especially after you left," I said.

"I never meant to leave you or hurt you."

Tears filled my eyes.

(Dial tone)

"Hello?"

I guess he hung up. Thirty minutes later he let me know that his phone had died. I could not believe that even after all this time we could talk for hours like we never missed a beat. I was happy to feel a connection with someone, but I also felt guilty. Like I was cheating on my husband. I had to end this before it started. I must let it go. I would not answer his calls or text him back. It would break my heart, but if I let him in, there would be no room for me to fix things with my husband.

I decided after dinner I would make a special dessert and talk to my husband about our marriage and how we can make things better. I know we really need to change our living situation, so we came to focus on us. I decided to head to the store before he got off so I could get things together before he came home. As I was shopping my phone was blowing up. My aunt, granny, and mom were calling. I finally answered.

"Ke!!!"

"What's up Tiff?", I asked.

"Marq got stabbed, he on the way to the hospital," she said.

"What??? What happened?"

"We don't know yet. Okay, I am going to see if I can get down there", I said.

I hurried to the cash register to check out. I slapped the groceries in my car and speed home. As I pulled up, I saw my husband's car. I guess today was an early day. I opened the door. Isis was in her playpen in the living room crying.

"Ahhh…. Ohh… Ummm", moaned Imani.

I dropped the groceries and walked down the hall. The moaning got louder.

"Yesss daddy…. OH", Imani screamed.

The door was cracked to the Smith's room. I knew Ryan wasn't off yet, so I peeked inside. My heart fell to the floor as I took in what I saw. Imani was bouncing on my husband's dick. I stepped back, this cannot be real. I looked again. Jason turned her over and started ramming her from the back as her screams got louder. I walked into my room and loaded the gun. These motherfuckers got me fucked all the way up. I'm about to set it off in this bitch. No bitch think, who gone take care of Jayden? You wanted out, this is out. My thoughts were coming in so fast. I grabbed my phone and recorded the scene. She was back on top riding him faster and faster. His hands were gripping her ass. She looked up and squeezed his chest as her body began to shake. His toes were curling. She screamed, and he groaned, they were cuming.

After they were done, I saved the video picked up the groceries and exited the apartment. I sat in my car and cried. I could not do anything else. After I gathered my thoughts, I picked up Jayden from the bus stop, and we entered the house. Ryan and Jason were playing the game, and Imani was sitting on the couch with the baby.

"Hey Ke," Imani said.

Hey, you trifling whore I thought. "Hey, I said what y'all up too?", I asked.

I looked at Jason. "Babe I need to talk to you," I said. I told Jason about my brother and that I would be going to Texas to support my family. Lord, I needed the strength to keep it together. He gave me a hug and told me he understood, and to take $400 out of the bank for the trip. I damn near puked feeling his body touching mine. How could he cheat on me with this bitch? I went to the room and packed mine and Jayden's bags. When I came out everyone was on the patio talking. I let Jayden watch cartoons as I made dinner.

I was making chili. I did everything as usual, as the meat was cooking, I went into the restroom. I shit in a cup. I added it to the chili and mixed it in.

"Dinner is ready," I said.

They all came in smiling. I smiled back. They sat at the dinner table. "Chili and cheese bread."

I grabbed our bags.

"Are you going to eat babe?", Jason asked.

"No, I think I am going to go ahead and get on the road, plus I need to get to the bank."

I kissed his cheek and said bye to everyone else. As I walked to the door, they began to swallow their food.

"Ke, this is good, I have never added corn to chili before," Imani said.

Corn? I thought. Oh yeah, we had taco soup a few days ago. "I just wanted to try something new," I said, "Y'all enjoy, bye!" I said with the biggest smile.

I went to the bank. Instead of taking out $400, I took out $2500 and cleared our savings of $8000. It's not much, but it will help me and my son get a fresh start. I wasn't going to Blueville. I was going to Austin with my aunt, Jayla. Jason had never met her before and wouldn't find me. She had dealt with a cheating, lying, dirty bustard before. I knew she would understand why I left. I called my mom after I left the bank. My brother was stable and was going to heal. He had been stabbed a few times in the chest but would live.

Breaking Out

Getting to my aunt's was a struggle, between the pee breaks, the crying, and taking care of Jayden. I had finally arrived at my aunt's house, after twenty-six hours on the road. My aunt ran out of the house and greeted us. She held me in her arms as I cried o her shoulder, I was still upset. I could not believe that after all we had been through this dude would cheat on me, and with his best friends' wife. I guess you can't put shit pass anyone nowadays. My aunt settled and Jayden in her guest rooms. She worked at Price University and had a large four-bedroom house all to herself. I am surprised my other family member did not think to come this way. That morning I woke up ready to start some shit.

Text to Ryan: *Good morning Asshole, while you were out drinking your wife was doing this. This is all your fault your sorry excuse of a man.*

Text to Jason: *If you were going to cheat on me, you could of at least choose someone that was better than me.*

Text to Imani: *After all the stuff I did for you, you choose to fall on my husband's dick. It's okay though, watching you eat my shit pleased my soul.*

I attached the video I had recorded to all the messages. Five minutes later my phone was blowing up. This brought joy to my heart. Their little worlds were crumbling as mine did. I blocked all their numbers and got up to start my day. They didn't give up though. They started calling from block numbers. Jason was apologizing, then he was complaining about the accounts. Imani wanted to fight. Apparently, I had ruined her relationship. Ryan didn't respond, I bet his heart was broken, he was collateral damage. I cut my phone off and went down to talk to my aunt.

"How are you feeling today?", she asked.

"I am still in shock. It hurts, but better to find out now than waste any more time with him. Not to mention, the military lifestyle was not for me."

"You will be alright. We need to talk about the house rules", she said. "No coming in at all hours of the night, no locked doors, since you are here, I need you to keep the house clean every day, and I will charge you $500 a month for yall to stay."

Damn, I would better off getting my own spot I thought. Aunt Terri was a businesswoman, but I really needed a break. After living with my aunt, a few months things got unbearable. I was appreciative of the help, but the nagging and chores got old. I had found a job cleaning at Quinta Inn on the weekends, but it was not working. My boss was an asshole, and the customers were disgusting. Plus, with the hours I worked, I missed every football game my son had. The only good thing was I met Yvette. On my first day of working, Yvette yelled at me in front of everyone for over piling my cart with dirty laundry. She stayed on my case about everything. I almost quit because of her, but as I got to know her, she quickly became a person I felt I could talk to. During our breaks, we would always talk. I told her about my relationship with my mom, my abandonment issues, friendships, and my cheating husband. She was always there to listen, she never complained.

"Kennadi I will be leaving soon. I am going back to Illinois to stay with my son. I realized I am getting older and I want to be near my family", said Yvette.

"What?", I said. I hugged her. "I am going to miss you!"

"I will miss you too."

"You know you the only reason I kept this job."

"You will be alright," she said with a laugh.

"After all, I told you are you sure about that?"

"You come to me every day and tell me different stories about your past. You always tell me how people hurt you or how you feel you were set up in life from the beginning", she said.

"I know I just-," I started.

"Look you always say what others did, but my perspective is you allowed it. You allowed people to mistreat you, use you. You compromised yourself for others and loss you along the way", she said.

I stood there. I really did not know what to say.

"Kennadi, you need to take accountability, not everything that has happened to you is someone else's fault, you played a part as well. You are strong, you have been through some things, but those things only make you stronger."

"I don't want to be strong, I want to be happy," I said.

"You can be both. Don't let your past define you. Each day is a gift. You can wake up and recreate yourself at that moment. You may be lost now, but you will find your way."

She gave me a hug and left the room. She left me with my thoughts, and they were everywhere. Yvette was right. All this time I had been blaming everything that had happened to me on others. I was mad at my mom, my friends, my husband. I refused to look at myself, view myself and actions from another perspective.

After Yvette left, I found another place to work. It was still a cleaning job, but the pay was better, and I could work overnight so I would be able to spend time with Jayden in the day. It wasn't easy. There were nights I would cry as I cleaned. My back was hurting, I was tired, and even though it paid more than my last job taxes were eating my check. What didn't go to taxes went towards my credit card debt. The entire time I had been with Jason, I couldn't work, but we needed things. I had to pay for school registration, clothes, food, and shoes for him. Jason had refused to buy certain things because he felt like he paid for enough. I didn't want my child to be without, or to be bullied because he didn't have what others did. The money I had taken from Jason was dwindling. Also, I decided to keep the baby, and I was now four months pregnant, the baby would be here before I knew it. I needed this job. As I was working one-night, my aunt called.

"Ke, your mom looking for you. I think something is wrong with your grandfather", she said.

I had changed my number so Jason couldn't reach me. I was scared to give it out because I didn't want anyone to give it to him. A few months had passed since I left, but I was still paranoid. I called my mom from the office phone.

"Hello?"

"Ma?"

"Ke, how are you?"

"I'm alright ma," I said."

"Jason was looking for you. Is everything okay?"

"Yeah ma, I am at work, what's up?"

"PaPa is not doing well, we in the hospital right now. He has lost a lot of weight and is struggling to eat", she said. "Hey, can you video chat?"

"Yeah," I replied.

I hung up and called her via video chat on hangouts. I saw her, my aunt Tiff, and Aunt Diana sitting in the room. She panned the video over to my grandfather. I hardly recognized him. He had lost so much weight his skin was sagging on his face. His eyes were yellow, and he looked so tired. I fought back the tears, I didn't want him to see me cry. I tried to be strong for him. I spoke to my grandfather, he just smiled and waved. The room was quiet; I saw a nurse come in. Mom panned the camera around and told me she would call me back. I immediately hung up and sobbed. He was in the hospital many times before, but something was telling me this time it was different. I cleared my eyes and pulled out my camera. I made a video for my grandfather.

"Hey PaPa,

I know you have been in the hospital before, but the way everyone is acting, I know something is wrong. I just wanted to say the things I should have said to you a while ago. Thank you for everything you have done for me. You have been there for me through from the beginning. From taking me to see my mom, to towing cars, from basketballs to babies. I appreciate everything you have ever done for me, and I love you!", I said

I saved the video and cried. I wasn't ready to lose him. However, it didn't matter what I wanted, two days later he passed.

Surprise Visitor

I was able to take off work and make it to Blueville for my grandfather's funeral. When we arrived, I met my mom at my grandfather's house. All the family was there. I walked in the house, it looked more like a party to me. Music was blasting, and many people were drinking, I guess people grieved in different ways. My mom was in the back room.

"Hey man!", I said. She was a mess. Her eyes were red, and her hair was a mess. She was laying across the bed in a t-shirt some old torn pajama pants. I knew my grandfather's death would hit her hard. She was a daddy's girl.

Jayden ran to her, "Hey granny!", he said.

She sat up and squeezed him tight. "Hey yall," she said in a somber voice.

I looked around the room, then ran outside to get some air. I couldn't breathe. Reality had slapped me in the face he was really gone. I broke down sobbing.

"Ke?", a deep voice called my name.

I turned around, it was my brother I squeezed him so hard. I had not seen him in a while. After the stabbing incident, he ended up going to jail for possession of an illegal substance. They released him so he could make it to the funeral. After I pulled myself together, we sat on the back of the car to reminisce about our grandfather. It was getting late, so I went to get Jayden, so we could check into the hotel and get ready for the funeral tomorrow.

The funeral was nice. My grandfather looked good. He wore a red shirt and his overalls. I was happy they dressed him as he was and not in some tacky Easter Sunday suit. Everyone wore red and black to honor my grandfather. During the service, many people told stories of how he helped them in their time of need. There was also a part of the ceremony where my cousins presented his motorcycle jacket and helmet and marched it to his casket. As people walked around to view the body. A beautiful thick woman approached me. My emotions were already everywhere, and seeing her did not help. Niya. She hugged me tightly.

"I am sorry for your loss," she whispered and kissed my cheek.

I just squeezed her. As she turned to leave, I caught a glimpse of her family. She was married and had a little boy now. I couldn't help but feel the tug from my heart as she walked away.

After the funeral, we were supposed to go to the church the family could be served lunch. I was wearing a dress and heels. I wanted to get comfortable before I went anywhere else.

"Mom, can you take me by the hotel, so I can change?"

She nodded her head. We arrived, and I ran into the hotel. I entered the room key and started pulling off my dress.

"So, you thought you could just leave me huh?"

I turned around, and Jason was walking out of the bathroom. "What are you doing here," I said walking backward.

"Why did you leave? You didn't even give me a chance to explain?"

"I saw what I saw, Dammit I recorded it. There was nothing to explain", I said.

"We were going through, I messed up, you didn't give me a chance," he said, "I love you."

"Jason, I know my worth. You were loving me when you were fucking her? Why are you here? You had to know there was no coming back from that", I said.

"I came to get what's mine."

"I don't have your money. I spent it", I said.

"I don't want the money. You can't leave me, we are married. To death do us part", he said. He pulled out a gun from behind his back.

"I … Please… Don't do this …What about Jayden?", I asked. I was so happy Jayden was not with me right not. He had ridden to the church with my grandmother and his cousins.

"He will be with me," he said.

He walked up to me and punched me in the stomach. I fell to the floor. I couldn't breathe. I heard the gun cock back. I closed my eyes. "Lord forgive me!", I said

(Pow)…………. (Pow Pow Pow)

This was it. I was dead I thought. I opened my eyes. Jason had fallen to his knees, then fell to the floor behind me. I looked up to the doorway. It was my mother. She was still pointing the gun.

"Ma, Mom. She didn't move. It was like she was stuck. "I think she was in shock.

I eased up to her and lowered the gun.

"I had too," she said, He couldn't do it again.

"Again? Mom, what are you talking about?"

"Your dad, he couldn't do it again," she said.

"Mom? You're not making sense."

Butterfly

We did not make it to lunch. My mom was arrested and had now ended up in the same place she was before. Jacho Women's Penitentiary. The trial went by quick as she pleaded guilty this time. Today was the day I could go see her. When I arrived at the prison, I already knew what to expect. I sat down at the old white picnic table waiting for my mom to come out.

"Ke!"

"Hey ma." I ran and hugged her. She looked so much better than she did at the funeral.

We sat down, and I updated her on my life and how things were going with Jayden and me. We now lived in San Antonio, Texas. After my husband's death, I received an insurance check of $75,000. This offered me a chance to move out of my aunt's house and start completely over.

"How's the baby?"

"I lost it," I said. When Jason kicked me in the stomach, the placenta separated from my uterus. "Mom I need to ask you something. What did you mean when you said My dad, he couldn't do it again?", I asked.

"Ke. I never told you, but your dad tried to kill me."

"When?"

"The night he died," she said, "It started out as a get-together. It was me, your dad, aunt Tiff, and her boyfriend, Carl. Granny had gone out of town, and we invited our boyfriends over."

I nodded.

"I remember, because I was frying chicken and it never cooked all the way through, it was bloody. I gave up and popped open some Moonshine. We all got so drunk. Your dad and Carl wanted to play Russian Roulette, me and Tiff stopped them. Tiff and Carl went into her room while your dad and I were sitting on the couch. He told me he needed to tell me something. He had cheated on me a while back and had another little girl."

"Kaydence," I said.

"Yes. Ke my heart was broken. I told him to leave, He refused, he told me he wasn't going anywhere. I slapped him and started punching him, he grabbed the gun from the table and smacked me across the face with it. My head started to bleed. He then kicked me in my stomach. I managed to get up, and we started fighting with the gun."

"It went off?", I asked.

"Yes, in the struggle. Your dad fell to the floor. He was bleeding from his stomach. I called 9-1-1, but it was too late. He was dead when they got there."

"If that is what happened wasn't its self-defense?", I asked

"Yes, but I felt so guilty. I volunteered to take the time. I wanted to get away and needed to be punished", she said. She was sobbing.

I put my hands on hers. "It's okay ma. Thank you for saving me", I said.

The next day after I dropped Jayden off at school, I picked up the picked up the ashes. I put some of them in a cross necklace. I wanted to give them to Jayden when he got older, something to remember his dad by. After I was done, I had a few words to say to him on my behalf.

Jason, I do not know how we got here, but I am glad we did. I was willing to lose myself to please you. I loved you the best way I knew how, and you broke my heart into a million pieces. I don't regret meeting you. You taught me what I don't want in my life, you taught me that no matter who came into my life, never to compromise myself. Because of you I have now know what I want and will accept nothing else. I have learned I do not need you or any other man to fill the hole in my heart. I will fill that hole by taking care of myself. I have shed that skin and broke out of that dark place, climbed out of that cocoon and became a butterfly. I have learned to flap my own wings and soar all on my own. So, thank you.

I went into the bathroom and flushed his ashes right down the sink. That chapter was closed, and I was ready for the next one, whatever it may bring.

Epilogue

Six months later Kennadi committed suicide. She drove her car off a bridge. She felt like she could not live anymore and ended it all, with one quick turn. She took Jayden with her. Due to her past, she felt no one could take care of him the way he deserved. You see looking back through Kennadi's story you will notice how she focused on the unfortunate events in her life. She rarely spent time speaking about the good. Her family was not perfect, but they loved and cared for one another. Her mom may have said some hurtful things, but she always provided for Kennadi and did her best to show Kennadi she loved her. Kennadi's friends did not abandon her, but because she had abandonment issues, she felt alone even in their presence. Kennadi had struggled with the battles in her mind for a long time. She struggled with rejection, self- esteem, fear, and being alone. Even after getting a chance to start over, she could not escape the darkness in her mind. Initially, she thought she was strong enough for a new start, but withered away from the inside out. No matter what she tried to do, she could not escape her past. Many people believe that mental health issues are not real. They say you can control yourself or you just want attention they say. You reach out for help, and people ignore you or tell you that you are being dramatic until they are sitting at your funeral.

Becoming A Butterfly

Love and Hate,

influenced my fate.

Abandonment, depression, abuse,

added to my issues.

In denial.

I knew right from wrong, rules and laws.

I did what I wanted,

blamed others for my flaws.

I ignored advice,

blocked out all light.

I wasn't' scared,

I was comfortable there.

No one expected anything from me.

They expected the worse.

I was fine with that,

I had accepted my curse.

Until my thoughts took over,

battle in my mind.

Death was an option,

trust me, I had tried,

but something told me to look up and climb.

Climb out of the darkness,

out of my head.

Climb out of the rumors

about who was in my bed.

Climb out of the criticism,

and away from people telling me my life was over.

Climb away from the past,

that time was over.

I would climb to a place,

filled with peace.

Happiness, joy, and freedom,

would surround me.

I would be uncomfortable at first this was something new,

but change and growth were long overdue.

I realized my flaws.

Climbed out of that cocoon.

Next season, I will be a butterfly,

can't wait 'til flowers bloom.

KeArra Robinson

Letter to Readers

Dear Readers,

For most of my life, I believed I was what and who those around me said I was. I never took the time to figure out the person I wanted to be until I lost myself completely. I had spent most of my time trying to fit in or meet everyone else's expectations. I rarely asked myself what I wanted or whom I wanted to be. I felt that life started me out at a disadvantage and there was no way to come back from that, but I was wrong. I am now almost 30 years old and just now realizing that I could change my situation, that I am in charge of what happens to me, by choosing how I want to be treated and what I will allow. I realized it's not too late to make a fresh start, to get the help you desperately needed when you were younger. I wasted years of my life worrying about what others would think of me, requiring approval, and trying to stop the gossip surrounding myself and my family. The truth is, people are going to talk about you no matter what you choose to do in life, you will never be good enough in their eyes. Therefore, you must live for yourself, make your own decisions, decide what makes you happy, and go after it. If you need help reach out for it. Do not live for everyone else, live for yourself.

KeArra

Remember, you are not ALONE!

Child Abuse Hotline................................ (800) 422-4453

National Domestic Violence Hotline......(800) 799-7233

Substance Abuse and Mental Health Services Administration (SAMHSA)......................(800) 662-4357

Children & Adults with Attention Deficit/Hyperactivity Disorder Resource Center (CHADD).......(800) 233-4050

Suicide Prevention Lifeline......................(800) 273-TALK

Trevor HelpLine / Suicide Prevention for LGBTQ+ Teens
....
....(866) 488-7386

Crisis Text Line..............................Text HOME to 741741

Rape, Abuse, Incest, National Network (RAINN)... (800) 656-4673

More information can be found at this link:
https://www.healthyplace.com/other-info/resources/mental-health-hotline-numbers-and-referral-resources

Discussion Questions

1. What did you learn or admire most about this novel?
2. Why do you think Kennadi could only see the bad in her life?
3. Do you think the situation of Kennadi's parents crippled her outlook on life??
4. Was she too hard on her mom?
5. After time served, do you think Ms. Kassie still struggled actions the night Kennadi's dad passed?
6. Do you think the deaths in Kennadi's life influenced her outlook on life?
7. Can you relate to any of the situations Kennadi went through?
8. Do you think Kennadi still loved Niya or Darnell? Or were they her comfort zone to escape the things going on in her life at the time?
9. Do you think Kennadi left Jason at the "right" time? Should she have given him a chance to clarify the situation?
10. Does Kennadi share similar behaviors to someone you know?
11. Do you think Kennadi would have committed suicide if she received professional help at a younger age?